Nancy-

The Roses of FELDSTONE

a regency romance

So lovely to meet you in Dallas! Enjoy

The Roses of FELDSTONE

a regency romance

ESTHER HATCH

Covenant Communications, Inc.

Cover image: *Woman Looking at Mansion* © Lee Avison / Trevillion Images

Published by Covenant Communications, Inc.
American Fork, Utah

Printed in the United States of America
First Printing: August 2018

24 23 22 21 20 19 18   10 9 8 7 6 5 4 3 2 1

ISBN 978-1-52440-589-2

To my mother,

who introduced me to the city library, the bookmobile, and the paperback book exchange. Thanks to her, books lined the walls of our basement and carpeted the floor near our beds. We didn't grow up surrounded by luxury. We grew up surrounded by books.

ACKNOWLEDGMENTS

THIS BOOK LITERALLY NEVER WOULD have been written if it weren't for my writers group—Paula Kremser and Alice Patron, thank you for being there every week! Laura Rupper, Tammi Bird, Monique Bird, Audrey Mangum, Josie Chilton, Lindy Hatch, Jen Hatch, Brook Andreoli, Lisa Kendrick, April Young, Karin Smith, Heidi Maxfield, Lora Jean Buss, Carrie Westover, Shauna Swinyard, and Lisa Rowley. Thanks for your critiques and inspiration. You read my novel when it was just a Google doc and covered it in much-needed comments. Every time someone read and enjoyed it, I was encouraged to keep going. A huge shout-out to Kim Dubois, who took the time to do some amazing copyedits before I submitted my manuscript to the publisher. If she didn't know what a run-on sentence was before she started, she certainly did after.

To my four boys—Logan, Christian, Vincent, and Everett—thank you for making me want to be productive in my free time and for putting up with me when I was absorbed in finishing just one more scene.

Thank you, Greg, for saying, "There was never any doubt," when my manuscript was accepted for publication. Everyone should have someone who believes in them like that. Sorry I gave you mono.

Thank you, Covenant Communications, for taking a chance on me.

And finally, I want to thank anyone who reads this book. My plan for *The Roses of Feldstone* is to bring a few hours of enjoyment to you. I didn't really think this book was going to change anyone's life—but in the end, it changed mine. Thank you for reading it!

"Is love a tender thing? It is too rough,
Too rude, too boist'rous, and it pricks like thorn."

—Romeo (Shakespeare, *Romeo and Juliet*, Act I, Scene IV)

CHAPTER 1

I SHOULD HAVE BEGGED MY parents to let me stay in London with Elizabeth.

The air in the carriage thickened as we rolled up the familiar birch-lined driveway of Feldstone Manor, William's home. I tried to draw in a deep, calming breath, but no matter how hard my lungs pulled, they didn't seem to fill properly. My parents and I had spent four tedious hours smelling each other's sweat and tasting the same dust with this destination in mind, and yet, if I were given the choice, I would turn the horses around and happily sit through four more hours if it meant I could return to London.

At least at the moment, Mama wasn't complaining about the travel conditions. Country roads were more poorly maintained than those in London. This didn't shock me, but it never ceased to amaze Mama. However, right now, she had given up her rant about the state of the roads so she could gripe about what the long drive had done to her hair.

I reached up to assess the state of my own hair but quickly jerked my hand away. It didn't matter what I looked like; I wasn't trying to impress anyone.

"Rose," my father said, interrupting my mother's tirade for a blessed moment. "Can you get this blasted dog off of my foot?"

I bent forward, trying to ignore the way my stomach revolted at the motion, but my mother beat me to the wrinkled ball of tan fur.

"Oh, you poor thing!" Mama said in the sickeningly sweet voice she used only with Daffodil. She lifted up her pug—named after her *favorite* flower—to eye level, touched its nose to her own, and then placed the dog on her lap. "I know how much you hate carriage rides, but it will all be worth it in the end." I tried once again to take a deep breath of the dense air, but to no avail. I could manage only shallow puffs.

Daffodil had slept through all but five minutes of the journey before rising on her fat little haunches, looking out the window at the forested view, sighing, and going back to sleep. I, on the other hand, had felt nauseated since the city of Wycombe.

This was always the worst part, I reminded myself—seeing William for the first time. Every jostle of the wheels over the impressive stone-paved courtyard brought me closer to him, and I wasn't ready. Over the course of the drive, I had spent too much time thinking of what I would say to him, but now that we were almost there, everything seemed to flee from my mind. I leaned forward in order to look past my mother and out the window. As much as I wished my parents hadn't dragged me here, the first view of Feldstone Manor was always breathtaking.

It was just so immense. Its size was always shocking, even though this was our fourth visit. Moss grew on some of the main-floor stone, and it only added to the sense of long-established grandeur. The east and west wings were lined with windows on all three floors, and the main entrance of the home boasted an intricate stone archway. Every time the butler struggled to open the massive wooden front door, I was reminded that nothing was done by halves at Feldstone. If a larger door could have been opened, it would have been installed there. The manor was as formidable as it was timeless. I counted on it never changing, but today, something *was* different.

"Oh, Sir John!" my mother exclaimed, grabbing my father's hand to make sure he was paying attention to her. She seemed to think that was the only way to assure his attention, and she was probably right.

"Look at the changes they have made since we were here last year! It must be so nice to have twelve thousand pounds a year to make such improvements."

My father looked out the window and obligingly gave a small grunt.

I followed my mother's gaze to make sure she was looking at the same change I had seen. "Do you mean those ghastly lions they have placed on either side of the entrance?" I asked. "I am not certain I would call that an improvement."

"Oh, Rose"—she shushed me—"you only say that because they replaced those old rosebushes. *Anyone* can have rosebushes, but not everyone can commission such fearsome statues."

"But they were the only soft feature anywhere near the entrance of the home," I reminded her. I wouldn't put it past William to have gotten rid of the roses to spite me. He knew how much I adored those bushes, and the lions really were appalling. He couldn't have found anything I hated more to replace the roses. Once again, I lamented the day my father and the earl had become fast friends during a hunting trip with a mutual acquaintance.

The family must have been alerted to our arrival, for the Earl of Chatsworth exited his home to greet us. Towering directly behind him was William. William had been tall since I had known him, but he seemed larger, broader, and more unyielding today. He had lost his softness, just as his home had. I tried not to notice the way his arms filled out his well-tailored jacket. It was a reminder that he had grown older and more powerful. He was no longer the young man I had first met. I couldn't see his eyes from this distance but knew they would still be the same gray eyes that seemed to read my every thought—and then judge me for them.

If only he weren't so good-looking, perhaps we could get along, I thought. I tried to remember all the barbs I had been practicing on the long ride here, but sure enough, they had fled. I blamed the lions. It was a brilliant move on his part, to throw me off like that.

A footman took my hand as I grasped my rumpled gray traveling dress and descended from the carriage. Compared to William's crisp, immaculate appearance, I already felt at a disadvantage. Ahead of me, my mother's pug escaped her arms and ran right up to the base of one of the stone lions to relieve herself.

"Daffodil!" my mother exclaimed in horror as she shuffled quickly over to her silly dog.

I smiled slightly. Maybe it was time I gave that dog another chance. She obviously shared my taste in decorations.

I measured the space between myself and the entrance to the home. Just ten more steps and I would be next to William, and I still couldn't manage to recall a single one of my well-thought-out disparaging remarks. I squared my shoulders. I was eighteen now, not a young, naive fifteen-year-old. I curtsied to his father, and then made my way to William. The curtsy I gave him was more of a cursory bob. I would have hated for him to think I respected him in the least.

"Rose," he said as I looked up from my curtsy-bob. He looked down at me with his awful smirk that had been driving me to distraction for three years. Well, really, just the past two. Our first year together had been filled with genuine smiles. "It's pleasant to see you again."

See me! Not be with me, not talk with me. As if he hoped he would only have to glance at me once in a while from a distance throughout the five-week stay.

Something witty. Something stinging. Something . . .

"William," I replied.

His smile deepened, creating distracting lines on either side of his mouth. His gray eyes seemed to spark with amusement. He must know how hard I worked to come up with scathing replies to anything he said. "You must not find all roses pleasant though," I said, not willing to be at such a disadvantage so early on in the visit. "Seeing as you had your front rose garden removed. It is too bad. They were one of the few things to love in this household." This last part I said more quietly, not wanting to distress his father, the earl.

William just shrugged, his shoulders making a lazy journey upward. "They were diseased," he replied.

Everyone else was moving into the house, and William and I were alone at the back of the group, so no one would notice if I put my hands around his neck and squeezed. Just a little bit, just enough to scare him. I was staring at his neck, and he must have noticed because he chuckled before saying, "Come in, Rose."

We shouldn't have called each other William and Rose. He was Lord Telford, and I was Miss Davenport. Now that my four elder sisters were married, there was almost no use for my given name anymore. But we had met when I was still young enough that calling each other by our Christian names wasn't scandalous, and our fathers had insisted on it. They'd said that with how often we planned to visit, we should act more like cousins.

It really was time we stopped though. I had come out two seasons ago, so as inappropriate as it had been in the past, it was even more so now. More than that, though, it was a constant reminder that William still thought of me as a young girl. If he had felt that it was truly inappropriate, he would have stopped. William was nothing if not proper.

William reached for my elbow to escort me in, and I pulled away. I could make it up the three steps to the doorway without his assistance. I heard him sigh and then listened to the crunch of his footsteps as they followed mine.

Ahead of us, Lord Chatsworth was telling my father about the new firearm he had purchased.

My mother was busy verifying with the housekeeper that she had the same room as last year. "It is the one that gets the most sun in the morning," she said.

Five weeks, I thought. I would be in his household for five weeks. I had done it before, and, saints help me, I would be doing it again next year. I just needed to suffer through it. And for heaven's sake, I needed to figure out how to hold up my half of an intelligent conversation.

I was shown to my usual room, and a footman delivered my trunk. Lydia, my borrowed lady's maid, rifled through my gowns, occasionally pulling or shaking one to try to remove the creases from their journey. "I will only have time to iron one gown before you join the others in the drawing room. Which gown would you like to wear for dinner, miss?" she asked.

"The mauve one," I replied. The mauve dress was a hand-me-down from my older sister Elizabeth, but it looked as though it had been made for me. It somehow made my eyes look two shades greener. It was lower cut than most of my evening gowns but not so low as to be scandalous. After the gown was ready, Lydia started working on my hair. I smiled as I watched her dexterous hands wrap locks of my hair on top of my head in intricate patterns. She was one of my favorite things about visiting Feldstone Manor. She was as pleasant as my own lady's maid at home but infinitely more skilled with her hands. As frustrated and embarrassed as I was with my mother for economizing by not bringing Johanna, I really did love having Lydia work on my hair.

With emerald drop earrings dangling from my ears and my dark hair piled up on my head, I glanced into the mirror. My cheeks didn't need any pinching; my face was flushed enough as it was. "Why don't you stand up so I can look you over?" Lydia asked. I stood from the chair, which made me almost a foot taller than her. She was petite, and I was, as my mother put it, "unusually large." In truth, I was not large—just tall. I had no hips to speak of. The only curves I could boast of were, at best, adequate.

"You look majestic," Lydia said. "It is always fun to have such a beauty to dress."

I smiled at Lydia in thanks and then practiced that smile in the mirror for a moment. I was suddenly feeling better about the evening ahead of me. I was headed to battle, and this ensemble was my favorite armor. With one more thank-you to Lydia, I turned and walked to the door.

I entered the drawing room with my head poised. My father and Lord Chatsworth sat in leather club chairs near the grand fireplace. Although they were nearly polar opposites in appearance—my father was shorter and heavyset, with dark features, and Lord Chatsworth was lean and tall—they had one thing in common. It was what had brought them together in the first place: the love of the hunt. Although I couldn't hear their conversation, I knew they would be discussing what hunting excursions they would find most enjoyable over the course of the next few days. Mother was composing a letter at the writing table, most likely letting my eldest sister know we had arrived safely. William stood next to the bookshelf, his head bent over a book. Father and the earl set aside their papers and stood to greet me, my father giving me a proud glance.

"My, Rose, don't you look lovely this evening," my father said. "She has grown even more beautiful this year. Isn't that true, Chatsworth?"

"Most definitely," the earl replied dutifully.

"Thank you both," I replied, still standing in the doorway, not certain where to pass the time until dinner was announced.

William hadn't even looked up.

The men sat back down, and I decided not to join them or my mother but to walk over to where William was reading. I wanted to see what was so captivating that he would forget common etiquette, and I hadn't put on all this armor for nothing.

"What book is it that has you so enthralled, William?" I asked. He surprised me by snapping the book closed and balling his right fist as if he were hiding something there. Maybe I had been wrong; perhaps he hadn't been reading at all.

"Rose," William said, putting his right hand behind his back. It was most likely a trap, but I couldn't help but fall into it.

"What are you hiding?" I lowered my voice. "Something scandalous?"

He scoffed and looked at me, eyes widening slightly at the sight of my neckline. He took a half step back. "Of course nothing scandalous," he replied.

"Well then, may I see it?"

"No," he answered, taking another short step away.

I stepped forward and grabbed his hand in a movement so fast no one else in the room could have followed it. I turned my body to block the view from our fathers as I tried to pry open his fingers.

"Rose!" he whispered quietly but with force as he backed away once again and pulled his hand away from mine. I felt something in his hand rub lightly on my palm as he pulled away.

Inspecting my hand, I saw a faint black smudge, and I knew exactly what it was. "Charcoal!" I announced in a triumphant whisper, holding up my hand as proof. "William, do you still draw?" I asked, surprised. Our first year here, I had discovered that William had a love for drawing the small animals he found in the garden. Each of his sketches was more amazing than the last, but I had to bribe him with stolen fruitcake for him to show me any of them. I had assumed after that first year that he had stopped to pursue more gentlemanly pursuits, but apparently, he hadn't. He just hadn't trusted me anymore with his secrets.

"Has Cook laid out any fruitcakes?" I asked him, wondering how well he remembered that first year.

"Please," he said. "It would take much more than my own fruitcake to convince me to show you what is in my sketchbook." I smiled. He was treating me like a child, but at least he remembered.

"Trifle?" I asked, and he chuckled.

"The contents of this book are worth more than a trifle to me."

"Ah yes, I suppose they would be." I sighed, looking longingly at his small sketchbook, remembering the way he had been able to make squirrels, hedgehogs, and dormice come to life with just a few strokes.

"Isn't there anything I could tempt you with to get a peek at what you have in there?"

William's gaze dropped to my mouth for half a heartbeat, but he quickly looked up and gave me his lopsided grin. "Sorry, Rose, nothing *you* have could tempt me to show you even a single drawing in this book."

I knew I wasn't tempting or even interesting to him. I didn't want to be, but still, it stung to hear it. "There was a time when you used to let me see your drawings," I protested, but it didn't move him.

"I let you see *some* of my drawings."

"I am quite certain you let me see most of them. That is, until you tired of me." Our eyes met for a moment, and I was transported back to our first magical year when we had been friends.

We had spent hours together in the garden, where he would draw and I would laugh in delight at the uncanny likeness of everything he chose to sketch. I knew William's older brother, Joseph, had always mocked him for drawing. I was the first person who had been so enthralled by what he could do with paper and a little bit of charcoal. That had all been before Joseph had run off though. During the beginning of our second annual visit, Joseph had come home from his tour of the continent one evening to announce that he had married a foreigner. In the midst of the upheaval in his household, he had just left. I had never liked Joseph much, and I liked him less now because of the way he had hurt his mother and changed his brother.

Determined to grow up overnight, William had stopped spending time with me in the garden. Later that year, when I had my come-out ball in London, he had been there, and although I had caught him glaring at me, he had never spoken to me or acknowledged our acquaintance. Sometimes I missed the old William, and if I were honest with myself, I would have to admit that all my goading was a way to get a rise out of him. Trying to see that old carefree friend, the man he had been before Joseph had run off to Spain and been disinherited.

"You followed me like a loyal little puppy that year. Is it any wonder I tired of you?" William said, startling me out of my reverie.

"I did a lot of things when I was younger, but following you around was not one of them." In truth, it was. "When you stay in the same house, you are bound to bump into each other now and again." Especially when I had known his schedule. "Besides, maybe you were the one following me around." William's right eyebrow rose in disbelief. I squared my shoulders and schooled my face into what I hoped was innocent confusion at his silent questioning.

I was done being a loyal pup to him. It took me most of one five-week visit and a London season to finally realize he wasn't going to stop ignoring me. I had held out hope that we would go back to the way things had been when we'd visited for Michaelmas last year, but William had been cold and indifferent. I despised being ignored, so I was probably the one who had started our ridiculous game of trying to best each other at insults.

"You really did do a lot of things when you were younger," he said. "I seem to recall you used to eat petit fours by the fours, claiming their name required it." His hand reached up to cover the corners of his mouth. "Your French was never stellar."

"It still isn't," I grudgingly admitted.

"That's not surprising. I'll make a special request and see that Cook has petit fours ready for tea. Perhaps you could fit four in your mouth at once."

"Perhaps I will."

"That would be a sight to see. I should invite some of the neighbors in. They will be impressed by the many talents of our visiting guest."

"Many talents, you say. What else would you have me do for entertainment?"

William set his book down on the shelf so he could pretend to seriously contemplate the question. I eyed the book. Maybe I could snatch it and catch a glimpse of what was inside.

"Do you still dig in the dirt?"

"No," I said in a harsh whisper, appalled that he would bring that up. I had done that only one time, after overhearing the gardener say that digging the dirt around the rosebushes would help them thrive. A filthy dress torn by thorns in multiple places resulted in my not being allowed outside for two days. I'd done a lot of tedious embroidery in those two days.

"Well, I can't invite guests over just to watch you eat petit fours. They would be bored to tears."

"You only say that because you haven't seen me eat petit fours recently," I said archly.

He laughed. A real laugh. It was short, almost like a cough that caught him by surprise, but still, it was not the scoff or derisive chuckle he usually reacted with when I tried to provoke him. The room seemed to brighten, as if a dozen newspapers had been thrown in the fire. It had been a long time since I'd made him laugh. I wanted him to laugh again.

"If you think that would be entertaining," I said, "you should see what I can do with a banbury cake. The neighbors would be talking about it for days." I tried, but to no avail. It looked like he regretted the first laugh, because now he was closing down. His face relaxed into the bored expression he so often wore while talking to me. His hand was reaching back up for his book.

"I don't think I am comfortable putting you on display like that, Rose. It would be highly inappropriate." He answered arrogantly, and the moment was gone.

"Well, I would hate to make *you* uncomfortable while entertaining *your* guests. Besides, I am quite certain nothing you could do with your mouth would be anywhere near that impressive." Whatever brightness was left in the room faded as soon as the unfortunate choice of words left my lips.

William's expression didn't change. If anything, he became even more still. I looked closely at his chest to make sure he was still breathing. It took a moment, but at last, it expanded with air. I had probably gone too far.

"And now I have made you uncomfortable . . ." I scrambled for something else I could say.

"Trust me, Rose," William interrupted my painful search for words. "Nothing would make me more comfortable than for us to finish this conversation. Perhaps there is a book here you would like to peruse so I can return to what I was doing earlier."

"Yes, I'll do that," I said, not knowing why I had decided to talk to the snobbish prude anyway. He obviously wanted to get rid of me as quickly as possible, and I was done talking to him too.

I ran my fingertips along the spines of the books on the shelves farthest away from him but hardly saw the titles in front of me. Before I could find a book to my liking, the butler called us in to dinner. I followed my mother into the dining room, only then noticing that

Lady Chatsworth had not joined our company. I had not yet seen her on this visit, and I hoped she was not ill. Ever since Joseph had run off, she had never been quite the same.

The ornately carved table was well stocked for our first evening here. The instant the variety of smells hit me, I was ravenous. I had only nibbled on food during our journey to Feldstone. Travel always suppressed my appetite. The few hours between our arrival and dinner had given me time to settle my stomach, and I was looking forward to eating a complete meal. All in small bites, of course. I needed to show William that despite my immature conversation earlier, I was very much grown up and able to eat like a lady.

I daintily nibbled at my food, despite my desire to eat at a quicker pace. The men were talking of the hunt they had planned for the morrow, but I noticed William didn't seem to be paying attention. I thought about reaching my foot under the table to kick his and get his attention as I had done at fifteen, but after my debacle in the drawing room, I decided against it.

"William," I whispered, not wanting to interrupt the conversation going on at the head of the table. He slowly turned his head away from his father, his wariness as obvious as a powdered wig.

"Don't worry, I promise I will not accost you with highly inappropriate conversation—"

"I hope when you are out in society in London you don't speak like you did earlier," he whispered fiercely, interrupting me. "It would lead to a sullied reputation, for certain."

"I never would, William," I said. "Please give me some credit. We both know we bring out the worst in each other." His gray eyes narrowed at my answer, and I wasn't sure if he was satisfied or unsatisfied by my answer. "I meant only to ask after your mother. Is she ill?"

His face fell, and he fumbled with his napkin. "She is under the weather today and has been for the last fortnight. With Michaelmas approaching, she always thinks of Joseph. I am afraid it is even worse this year."

"I'm sorry. Truly, I am." He didn't answer but instead reached for more pheasant.

"Will you be joining us on the hunt tomorrow?" my father asked William, and our whispered conversation was over.

"William isn't much of a hunter, is he?" my mother asked. "In the three years we have been coming to Feldstone Manor, I could count on one hand how many times he has joined you and Sir John in your sport."

"On the contrary, William is an excellent hunter, and we would love to have him join us," the earl said.

"I have rarely seen him hunt," my father said, "but the few times he joined us, he was definitely skilled. It seems to me that whenever we are here, he opts to stay at home with Rose."

William coughed slightly and then took a large drink of water.

Before he could reply, my mother interrupted. "What makes you say he stays here to be with Rose? William and I have had some quite scintillating conversations about ways Kent could improve the quality of entertainment available to those of rank." She sat straighter in her chair, obviously including our family in the ranked category, even though Father was only a baronet with a holding too small for much practical use. "Not to mention," she continued, "I have noticed he has enjoyed spending time with Daffodil. She is so diverting here in the country."

I caught William's eye and arched an eyebrow in question. He gave a small shake of his head. William's staying behind from the hunt to be entertained by Daffodil was as ridiculous as his staying away from the hunt to be with me.

William finally got a chance to reply. "I enjoy hunting with you, Father. Whenever Sir John is here, I have always assumed you would want to visit with each other and I would just be in the way."

"What? What would have given you that idea?" his father asked but then continued without waiting for a reply. "Well, you should come tomorrow. We could use a young pair of eyes as we hunt."

"I will think about it," William answered noncommittally.

I was fairly certain he wouldn't go. His excuse sounded unfounded. If he had liked hunting that much, he would have gone more often with our fathers. Heaven knew they hunted often enough during our stay.

CHAPTER 2

William went on the hunt.

Perhaps I shouldn't have been surprised, but I was. The main house seemed unusually quiet without the men around. The drawing room was never quiet as long as my mother was in it. But her conversation wasn't what I craved or even tolerated well for more than half an hour. After breakfast, I decided to head to the garden, where the stillness didn't seem quite so unnerving. Feldstone Manor gardens were some of the most diverse in all of Kent. The grounds had been painstakingly groomed, and the past few generations had improved the land by adding stone bridges across the stream that meandered through the wilder section of the land.

The stream wasn't as deep as it had been my first year. There had been more rainfall than usual then, but still, the sound of the water rushing over rocks reminded me of one of my first days here. I had been lonely and upset with Elizabeth for getting married, which had meant she couldn't come with us on the trip. I hadn't really been close to my three oldest sisters, but Elizabeth and I had come to rely on each other.

While wandering the gardens and bemoaning my fate, I'd heard the two Chatsworth brothers quarreling over William's drawings.

They were some of the most handsome young men I had ever met. Joseph, who had been Lord Telford at that time, was the type of man my older sisters would have swooned over. He was broad-chested, with boyish good looks. William had mostly just had the boyish good looks.

I didn't know either brother well, and I didn't think they would have liked me listening to their conversation, but they were blocking the path back to the manor. Rather than risk a meeting, I sought to leave quickly and quietly by wading through the stream.

If I had known the grounds better, I could have crossed at the bridge hidden by a grove of trees just upstream. They never would have heard me, and I could have escaped unnoticed. I often wonder how my relationship with William would have been different if I had done so. We might never have become friends. And despite all that had happened since, the thought chilled me.

My plan to escape might have worked, except I slipped on a rock and ended up falling with a splash into the swift-moving stream. I sat in the frigid water, not daring to move, while I listened to the sounds of the forest around me. Had they heard? The sound of their crashing boots made me realize they had. I struggled to at least get to a standing position before they arrived, but the rocks were moss covered and extremely slick.

"What the dev—" Lord Telford said. William hadn't said anything. He just stood there, looking at me. All I wanted was to get away from them. So I scrambled to my feet and continued my way across the stream.

"Don't do it," William said. "The stream is deeper than it looks. Come back this way, and we can help you to the house."

"I think I can make it," I said with more confidence than I felt. "I haven't been to the other side of the stream. I was hoping to explore it." And hoping to never see the pair of them again.

"You know, there is a bridge just twenty or thirty yards upstream," the older of the brothers yelled. "You could have just crossed there."

"Oh," I said, feeling foolish. "Thank you for the information. I will be sure to use the bridge on my way back."

I ignored the slippery rocks and continued to walk down the streambed. I was already wet anyway. The current was pulling at my skirts, and I slipped but righted myself with one hand on a boulder.

I heard splashing behind me; one of the brothers must have decided to come to my rescue, and I hoped it wasn't the big, handsome one.

I picked up my pace, even though the water was up past my knees. I slipped a second time, but this time, someone grabbed my arm. It was William. He didn't say anything but wrapped my arm around his. I expected him to take me back to the other bank, but to my surprise, he kept us wading away from his brother.

"Where are you going?" Lord Telford hollered.

"She wanted to go to the other side," William called out to him over his shoulder. The corners of his mouth crinkled in a devilish grin that made him at least as handsome as his brother. "So I am taking her to the other side."

"Well, aren't you kindness personified," Joseph called out.

William made no effort to respond to his brother.

With his arm steady next to mine, I managed to stay on my feet, and we reached the other side. We were both soaked, William from his knees down and me from my waist down. I knew we needed to get home as quickly as possible before one of us caught a chill.

"What did you want to see here?" he asked.

"What?"

"What was so interesting over here that it compelled you to wade across the stream to see it?"

I looked around the riverbank for anything that could have possibly tempted me here. It was beautiful, with moss covering the bottoms of the tree trunks, but so was the side we had just come from. I could see no reason I could have given as an excuse. "Nothing, I suppose," I said with a grimace. "I just wanted to get away from you and your brother."

He laughed. "Well, that makes two of us. Wanting to get away from Joseph, I mean. Sorry you are still stuck with me."

We laughed through chattering teeth as we made our way back—over the bridge this time—to the manor. It was the first time I had ever had a gentleman escort me anywhere.

We reached the front of the home, with my clothing soaked and his boots wet and muddy. He clipped a rose from the bushes by the front entrance, welcomed me to his home, and asked me to call him William. And because our fathers had asked me to as well, I did.

Now those roses were gone, torn out by the man who used to be the boy I cherished as a friend. We would never laugh together again like we did that day, crossing a stream so formally, with a bridge only a stone's throw away from us.

I kicked a rock into the stream and heard a satisfying plunk. My relationship with William was hopeless, but he wasn't the only member of the Chatsworth family I cared about. Lady Chatsworth lay sick in her bed, and I hadn't yet had an opportunity to see her. She had changed so drastically in the past two years. She had always wanted a daughter but was blessed only with two sons. My mother, on the other hand, already had four daughters before I was born four years after her last. I had always known my mother wanted to provide an heir for my father, and her pregnancy with me had been her last hope. I never felt neglected, but I hadn't really felt doted on until we'd come to stay at Feldstone Manor. Lady Chatsworth had been delighted to have a young lady visit in her home and had taken advantage of having me here.

I decided to cut short my visit to the flowers and the small animals that darted in and out of them. I knew Lady Chatsworth was not well enough to join our party, but perhaps she was up to having visitors. After a brisk walk back to the manor, I found Lydia and asked if she would talk to the housekeeper about my visiting Lady Chatsworth. I pulled open the heavy wooden door that led to my chambers and had to wait only a few moments before Lydia found me. Lady Chatsworth had told Lydia she would be happy to see me anytime this afternoon.

I rummaged through some of the accessory items Johanna had packed for me. One ribbon seemed to jump out at me. It was an old length Lady Chatsworth had bought for me when I was fifteen. Going shopping with her had been a dream come true for both of us.

William's mother had taken immense pleasure in shopping with me. There wasn't much available in Chatham, but she had managed to buy me some ribbon, a new bonnet, and some gloves. I still remembered the look on her face when, at the end of the visit, she had said, "If only we were in London, Rose. We wouldn't leave a thing on the shelves!"

I had dreamed of a London trip with her—not because of the fashionable gowns I would have bought but because of the time I would have spent with her, feeling like a precious daughter a mother would enjoy doting on.

Lydia knocked on the door a few minutes later. I asked if she would help me add the old ribbon to my coiffed hair, which, of course, she did masterfully. I thanked her before asking directions to Lady Chatsworth's room.

"'Tisn't far; it's the third door on the same side as Lord Telford's room."

"I am afraid I don't know where Lord Telford's chambers are," I said, trying to ignore the small bit of heat that rose into my cheeks.

"Oh, yes, of course you wouldn't. The family's rooms are also on the second floor, but on the exact opposite side of the manor. The south passageway at the back of the house will take you there. Turn left into the west wing hallway, and the first door you will pass on the right is Lord Telford's room. Lady Chatsworth's rooms are two doors down from his."

I found Lady Chatsworth's rooms without any trouble, though I couldn't help but look closely at William's door as I passed it. It was a solid wood door stained dark, just like the one that separated my room from the rest of the house, and yet somehow, his seemed more forbidding. The knots were deeper, and the lock seemed more intimidating. It was strange that after three visits, I hadn't ever known exactly where the family rooms were.

I knocked softly on Lady Chatsworth's door and then entered her chambers quietly. It was dim, but I could make out that a tray had already been set out on a bedside table. The table looked like it had remained in place by the bed for quite some time, even though by design, it was obviously meant to be temporary. Dark lavish drapes covered the windows, and matching curtains were pushed together in all corners of Lady Chatsworth's four-poster bed.

I smiled at Lady Chatsworth and curtsied low in hopes that she would notice me.

"Rose," she said. I could see movement on the bed. It looked like she was trying to raise herself up higher onto her pillows. "Come closer so I can see you." I walked over to her, but the light in the room was so faint I wondered how she would be able to see, even when I did reach the bedside.

"May I draw the curtains for you?" I asked. "It is a beautiful day outside." I waited for an answer that seemed too long in coming.

"I suppose so," she finally conceded. "But just a bit; the light is so bright."

I pulled the drapes open slowly so her eyes could adjust. When they were halfway drawn, I turned to Lady Chatsworth. It looked as though she had, at some point, been sitting up in bed, with pillows all around her, but she must have slowly sunk to a half-prostrate position. She closed her eyes in pain as they adjusted to the light in the room. I didn't feel guilty about opening the curtains though. The room felt cheerier already.

She opened her eyes as if the movement required great strength. But she smiled with a warmth that hadn't been present when I'd first entered the room. "Thank you, Rose. Usually William comes in by now and coaxes me into opening the drapes, but I haven't seen him yet this morning."

"He has gone hunting with the men," I told her, moving pillows around so I could help her to a more comfortable sitting position.

"Really? He usually doesn't go with them when you are here," she said.

I paused in the middle of fluffing a pillow and then pulled the edges of it apart extra tightly. So I hadn't just imagined that he stayed home most of the time. My father had mentioned it too, but I hadn't dared believe his words. Despite my satisfaction in being correct, I didn't want to talk of William. I wanted to find a topic other than her son, but other than Lady Chatsworth's health, which I didn't feel comfortable bringing up, he was the only thing that came to mind.

"How is your mother, dear?" she asked, and I was grateful she had found a safer topic. I sat on the side of her bed.

"She is doing well, as always," I said. It was my typical answer when asked about my mother, but as soon as I said it, I felt guilty. Lady Chatsworth's health seemed to only be getting worse.

"That is wonderful," Lady Chatsworth said. There was no artifice in her voice, and I was grateful she had never been one to find offense when it wasn't intended.

"Lady Chatsworth," I said with a sigh, "I have truly missed you. I wish you were able to come with us to dinner or join us on a ride during my stay." Her smile faded slightly, as if she knew that wasn't likely to happen. "Or perhaps we could try a quiet evening of cards." I didn't see how it would be possible to regain health, especially from a condition of the mind, without leaving her bed.

"I might be able to make it," she said. "I am feeling much better just seeing you this afternoon. Perhaps I will continue to feel better . . ." Her words trailed off, and she absentmindedly started smoothing the blankets surrounding her legs.

"I was in the garden this morning, and I walked across your bridge—the one with Lord Chatsworth's and your initials carved into stone. Some of the fall flowers were in bloom; it was so beautiful."

I was hoping to cheer her with the image, but her head fell back onto the pillows, and she closed her eyes with a sigh. "I had hoped that someday Joseph"—her voice caught on his name—"and his bride would carve their names into one of the stones near ours." I leaned forward so I wouldn't miss the rest of her thought. "Reginald would never allow it, even if Joseph did return from Spain."

"William will carve his name there," I said. Lady Chatsworth seemed to mourn the loss of her eldest son so much she neglected the one who had stayed by her side.

"Yes," she said, and her face relaxed into a soft smile. "William will. You are correct. And his children will, and perhaps one day, I will still see my Joseph and his children. I think Reginald would allow that. But their names will never be on the stone bridge."

"Joseph chose the path in life he truly wanted. I am sure it pained him to hurt you and Lord Chatsworth, but I think he must be happy in Spain. I am not certain he ever wanted the responsibility of caring for Feldstone Manor."

"I believe you're right, Rose, though I don't know how we all failed to see that side of him when you were able to see it in just the few weeks you stayed here." She sighed and looked more relaxed against the pillows. "William has always loved Feldstone," she added as an afterthought. I agreed with her but was surprised she would mention it.

Before William became heir, he had often talked to me about his plans. He would have inherited Campton House and its land in Surrey. It was one of the earl's smallest holdings—the only one that wasn't entailed. He had thought about going into the military or becoming a doctor. He much preferred the latter but felt that his parents wouldn't be comfortable having a doctor in the family. On the cusp of making that decision, the need had been whisked away. In truth, I didn't know how he felt about it, but even if he was happy to inherit the estate, he would probably never admit it, even to himself. I knew William well enough to surmise that he must feel like everything he would one day inherit was usurped from his brother.

Remembering the William of the past always left me with a strange sort of longing. That William no longer existed, but somehow, I always missed him. Lady Chatsworth was fiddling with her blanket and seemed lost in thought. I wondered what memory she was reliving. I asked her about the crop rotation this year, and she answered obligingly. Neither of us talked of her sons again and kept, instead, to other, more cheerful subjects. When it was time for me to leave, she seemed to be doing better. She didn't ask me to close the drapes, so I left them open. I got to the door and realized she had never asked about my hair ribbon, which saddened me. The Lady Chatsworth I used to know would have noticed.

I turned around because I thought speaking of it might cheer her. I knew I was happy reliving that memory. "Lady Chatsworth, I forgot to mention I found this ribbon in my reticule. Do you recognize it?"

Lady Chatsworth squinted her eyes, and I came closer so she could get a better look.

"Is that the ribbon we bought together?" she asked with a smile.

"Yes!" I said. "It is just as lovely as the day we bought it."

"That was a wonderful day."

"It was. Perhaps we could try a shopping trip again soon."

Immediately, her eyes glazed back over and her smile left. "Perhaps," she said, her eyes shifting from left to right until they landed on the bed. "Maybe when I have rested some more."

I gave her a wan smile. "If you ever feel up to it, I would love to join you." I made my way back to the door. "I will come visit you again soon."

"I would enjoy that," she said, closing her eyes and sinking deeper into her pillows. I quickly made my way out of the door, feeling the need to return to the garden and the sunlight and everything that was missing from that dreary room.

CHAPTER 3

TWO UNEVENTFUL DAYS LATER, I decided to visit Lady Chatsworth again. I had hoped she would have recovered enough to join us for meals, but she had continually stayed in her room. After a knock, I entered her room to find her in the exact same position I had left her in days before. The drapes were open, and I remembered that during our last visit, she mentioned William was usually the one to accomplish this task. He must have just left.

"Rose," Lady Chatsworth said, struggling to sit up. "Thank you for coming to visit with me. It gets rather dull just staring at these four walls." I wished she could see that nothing was stopping her from getting out of the room.

"I know we would all love to see you more often. I hope you will be feeling well enough to join us for dinner soon," I said as I hurried to her side. I moved some of the pillows around so she could sit up more comfortably.

"I would love to join you," she said, "but I think it may be awhile before I am up to it. It seems the more I rest, the more rest I need." I disagreed with her. More rest was the last thing she needed.

"Is there anything I could get for you?" I asked, but just as I was finishing my sentence, the door burst open, and William walked in with a large basket hanging from one arm.

"I have found the perfect basket, Mother . . ." he said, his last word trailing off when he looked up to see me already in the room. "Oh." His face fell. "Rose." He looked around, desperate for an escape. Even with the drapes open and his mother present, the room felt too dark and intimate for both of us to be here.

"I will leave you two alone," I volunteered, stepping away from Lady Chatsworth. Hopefully, my leaving would remove the panicked look from his face.

William visibly relaxed as he gave me a small nod. It seemed staying away from him was the most likely way to please him.

"Nonsense!" Lady Chatsworth protested with more strength in her voice than I would have thought possible. She reached for my arm to hold me there. "William is just here for a moment to show me the basket he chose to fill with some of our older nursery toys to send to Mrs. Wright. She just had her seventh baby, and I don't know when, if ever, this house will need them again." Her voice contained a deep sadness at that last part, and William sighed.

"Seventh!" I exclaimed. "William and I visited Mrs. Wright multiple times my first year here. She had only five then."

"You know the Wright family?" Lady Chatsworth asked. "That is wonderful. Could you help William pick out some of the toys from the nursery to bring her? I just don't feel up to leaving the room yet."

"I'm certain she wouldn't be interested," William said, opening the door wider and moving to the side in order to provide me ample space to walk past him as I left the room.

"I wouldn't be?" Or he didn't want me to be?

"No," William said. "I am quite sure the last thing in the world you would like to do is pick out toys for the Wrights." He gestured toward the door with his free hand.

"The last thing in the world?" I suddenly was overcome with the desire to see the Wright family again. I ignored William and turned instead to his mother. "I would love to help, Lady Chatsworth. You really shouldn't trust a man to know what toys a babe would like. Especially William; he was probably born serious."

"He was!" Lady Chatsworth laughed at that, which led to a small coughing fit, but when it calmed, she continued. "We used to make faces at him or tickle him to try to make him laugh, but all he ever wanted to do was stack blocks." I tried to picture William as a toddler. He still stood in the doorway, his cravat perfectly tied and his waistcoat buttoned up. Did he ever relax?

"Well, we won't send the blocks, then," I said. "Who knows when the urge to build might strike?"

"Mother, I am perfectly capable of picking out some toys to send to Mrs. Wright." A three-year-old couldn't have sounded more stubborn. It wasn't so hard to picture him as a toddler after all. "If it makes you feel better, I will bring them back here for you to inspect," William added. "Let's just let Rose get on with whatever she was doing."

"What I was doing and what I am doing now are two separate things. I haven't seen Mrs. Wright in two years. It will be very pleasant to see her again." William sucked in both his cheeks as if he were sucking on a lime. "Thank you for inviting me to join you on the visit," I said with an innocent smile, first to William and then to his mother.

"Visit? I never said anything about you coming with me!" he said, looking taken aback. "You were only going to help me pick out the presents."

Ah ha! He was going to let me help, then. "So you admit you need my help."

"No, I don't *need* your help to pick out toys or deliver a basket. I am perfectly capable of doing both on my own." I was sure he was capable, but he had let me see his hand when he'd made it so obvious he didn't want me to go with him. There was no chance I was staying home now.

"The nursery is on the third floor, isn't it, Lady Chatsworth?"

"Yes, William can take you there."

He was going to love that.

"Thank you, William," I said giving him a dazzling smile. "I haven't been to the nursery since my first visit to Feldstone."

William's jaw seemed to tighten, but otherwise, he stood perfectly still, everything in place, the perfect gentleman, cold and indifferent. With a small growl-like sound of frustration, he ran his free hand through his hair. Some of it tumbled forward onto his forehead. I felt the corners of my lip raise into a smile. Not so perfect now, was he?

"The Wright children are going to love what we picked out for them," I declared with a smirk as William and I walked toward the cottage. He hadn't talked to me the whole time we had picked out toys, though he had grunted a few times. A lady probably shouldn't take such delight in getting under a gentleman's skin, but I couldn't seem to help it. "No one was using them at Feldstone Manor anyway."

He continued to walk a few feet away from me, looking only forward, his face a grimace.

I knew my chatter annoyed him, so I kept it up. We had walked this road many times during our first year together. The Wrights had taken in a poor family whose father had been looking for work nearby. At that time, our baskets had been full of food, for it had been hard for the Wrights to keep so many mouths fed. I knew they and the Bensons had appreciated the practicality of the food, but it was fun to be bringing something more frivolous now that their situation had improved.

"Is that our apple tree ahead?" I asked William. I skipped forward a few steps in that direction. I had forgotten about the tree. When we'd been younger, we had often climbed it and brought fresh apples along with the bread and other foodstuffs Cook had packed. "Let's bring the Wrights some apples."

"No," William said firmly, finally breaking his silence.

"Why not? They always loved the apples we brought them."

"We are not stopping to pick apples. We are dropping off the basket as quickly as possible and then heading back home."

"It will only take a minute," I complained. Why was he so adamant about me not getting a few apples?

"The last time you climbed that tree, you nearly fell to your death. Let's just go."

"That's unfair," I said. "You were the one who dared me to climb that high. Besides, I would think falling to my death would be cause enough for you to want me to venture over there."

William just shook his head. He was back to being silent.

We walked a few more paces before he surprised me by continuing the conversation. "You shouldn't do something dangerous just because someone dares you to," he said. "It is a sign of low intelligence." Perhaps it was better when he kept his thoughts to himself.

"I would think that daring an impressionable fifteen-year-old to do something dangerous could also be seen as a sign of low intelligence," I fired back after a momentary delay. Sometimes I couldn't think of retorts quite fast enough, probably due to my *low intelligence*.

"You are just as improper as you have always been," he said. "You really shouldn't speak to a gentleman so boldly."

"But it is perfectly fine for you, a *gentleman*, to speak to me in the same manner?" I asked.

"It is not because I am a man. It is because I am older than you. At times, you might need reprimanding, and if I am the only one around to do it, I will." And he would delight in it, obviously.

"That is ridiculous, William. You never saw cause to treat me like this three years ago, and you were equally older than me then. And I am quite certain my behavior was far more improper as well."

I sped up, determined not to listen to William's insults any longer. The apple tree was several feet off the path, separated from the road by a sea of wild grasses. When we first visited here three years ago, William told me that in the spring, wildflowers bloomed all around the tree and blossoms filled the branches. I had longed to come back at that time of year to see it but had never had the chance.

I could see that there were still apples on the tree. I left the path and began to trudge through the grass, lifting my skirts slightly so they wouldn't snag. I had gone only about two steps when William took hold of my arm.

"No," he said again.

I whipped my head around. How dare he not speak to me all afternoon and then try to control me now. I tried to jerk my arm out of his grasp while I glared at him. "I am just going to get a few apples," I said. But he still wouldn't release my arm. "I won't climb very high. It wasn't until at least halfway up that the footholds became scarce, and there are probably some apples within easy reach anyway. I won't get hurt."

"I'm not stopping you because I think you will fall. I just don't want to spend one minute more than necessary on this errand."

"I won't even take a minute." I turned back to the tree.

"Please, Rose." His voice was quiet and serious and held just a note of the young man I used to know. "Don't go there."

I looked at the apples dangling from their branches. I knew they were ripe and begging to be picked. But William's tone felt like begging as well, and I couldn't disappoint him, not even after all this time. "All right," I said. "Let's just go visit Mrs. Wright."

We walked the rest of the way in silence. William never said why he didn't want me to pick the apples, and I never asked.

Just as we were about to arrive at the Wrights' cottage, William finally broke the silence. "Let's just drop off the basket and not go inside."

"Why would we do that? I haven't seen Mrs. Wright in two years," I said. "Of course we will go inside."

"It is just that—"

"You just want this visit to be over. I understand that, but you can't accuse me of being rude and improper in one breath and then ask me to be rude and improper in the next. It would be, well, rude and improper!" Sometimes irritation got the best of me.

"I would really rather not visit Mrs. Wright and her family with you," William said. His gray eyes were imploring me to agree with him. "The last thing I want to do is reminisce about old times."

We reached the door to her small, thatched-roof cottage, and I quickly rapped on the door before William could persuade me to change my mind. I didn't want to have another altercation with him, but I did want to see Mrs. Wright.

"You can head home, but I am going to visit with her," I said quickly, just as the door opened.

"Lord Telford! And Miss Davenport!" Mrs. Wright threw open the door in surprise. Her middle was rounder than when I had last seen her, but her mousy brown hair and broad smile were the same. "Miss Davenport, I haven't seen you in ages! My, you are even more beautiful than you were before!"

William and I stood there, holding our basket and smiling our broadest smiles, just like the unintelligent fools we were.

Mrs. Wright ushered me in, and to my surprise, William followed. I suppose he wasn't interested in offending our hostess after all. As soon as the door closed behind us, a small child of about two years came toddling up to Mrs. Wright. She leaned down and picked up the child without stopping her conversation.

"Miss Davenport, why haven't I seen you?" she asked. "Have you not visited in recent years? It is still Miss Davenport, isn't it? You haven't gone and gotten yourself married, have you?" At this juncture, I managed a small shake of my head before she was on to the next few questions. I didn't quite understand the point of asking so many questions if one didn't stop to listen for answers, but I remembered with a smile that it didn't seem to deter this woman. "What have you got there, my lord? A basket! Oh, you shouldn't have. Children, come look! Lord Telford and Miss Davenport have brought us a basket."

Five more children seemed to appear out of nowhere. I wasn't sure where they could have been hiding in the small cottage. The room we were in served as the sitting room. It was cluttered with Mrs. Wright's sewing and some well-used toys, but other than that, it was clean. I could see their open kitchen around the corner, where the family cooked and dined. I remembered from the Bensons' stay here that there were also two bedrooms. It must be much more comfortable now that the Wrights didn't have to fit their large family into only one of them. It was a small home, but it was filled with laughter, and I remembered why I had loved visiting here so much.

William set down the large basket and then chuckled when he was promptly covered in children. I recognized a few of them.

"Miss Mary!" I exclaimed. "You have grown so much since I last saw you! You are practically a young woman." Mary blushed, but before she could say anything, her mother piped up.

"She will be fourteen this year—not much younger than you were when we first met," Mrs. Wright said. I looked at Mary again. Had I really been that young? "She is growing to be quite a beauty, if I do say so myself," Mary's mother said proudly. "Although she has a far cry to go before she is as beautiful as you were that year, Miss Davenport. I have never seen such fresh beauty as you had then. Isn't that right, Lord Telford?"

William was down on one knee, helping the younger children pull toys out of the enormous basket. He paused for a moment, and then looked up at Mrs. Wright. "She was very beautiful that year; it is true," he said and then went back to helping the children.

The room seemed to brighten and grow warmer with William's words spoken so casually in front of Mrs. Wright. Would he have answered the question the same way if we had been alone? I was certain he wouldn't have.

"Not that you aren't beautiful now, miss. If anything, you are more beautiful, but it was such a unique sight to see such beauty at such a young age," Mrs. Wright said.

I desperately wanted to turn the conversation away from me. "Thank you, Mrs. Wright. That is sweet of you," I said. Protesting a compliment only seemed to lead to more compliments, so I quickly changed the subject. "Do you still have that kitten? Tiger? Isn't that what Mary named him?" He had been such a scared little thing when William and I had found him.

"He is outside and has grown quite fat," Mrs. Wright said proudly. "He has turned out to be quite the mouser. You probably wouldn't even recognize him."

"Oh, but may I see him?" Finding Tiger had been such an exciting moment that year. William and I had heard mewling on the roadside on our way to the Wrights. The poor thing had been half starved and terrified of us. When William had bent over to pick it up, the little striped kitten had arched its back and hissed but hadn't seemed to have the energy to run away.

I had quickly grabbed the cloth off our basket, taken the tiny mewing creature out of William's hands, and wrapped it up snugly. The kitten was fast asleep before we'd made it to the Wrights'. The Wright and Benson children had been so excited to see him that Mrs. Wright had given them permission to keep it. For weeks after that, we always made sure to bring extra milk for the family whenever we brought a basket.

"Tiger!" Mrs. Wright yelled as soon as she went out the back door. William, Mary, and I followed her, while the younger children remained with the basket of toys. I looked expectantly around but didn't see the striped cat anywhere. "He has a mind of his own now. He will only show up if he doesn't have anything better to do," she said.

"Oh, no. He will come, Mama, you'll see," Mary said.

I hoped Mary was right. I hadn't been allowed any animals of my own. I didn't count Daffodil; she was always Mother's pet. Tiger was as close as I had come to owning one.

"Do you still have your vegetable garden?" I asked as we waited for the elusive feline to show up. When I had been here before, the garden had been just outside the back door.

"Oh yes, we plant every year. Lord Telford suggested we move it to the side of the home; there is more sunlight there. He brings us seeds in the early spring and always knows just what to plant. I know he wasn't born to inherit Feldstone, but I feel that he has an uncommon talent for caring for the land. I know all the tenants have been very pleased with the improvements that have been made. They have been able to get higher yields than anyone remembers in the past."

"He even works in the fields with Papa during the harvest," Mary said. Her blue eyes were wide, and her hands were clasped behind her back. Her worship of William was more than apparent. I really hoped I had never looked at either William or Joseph that way when I was her age, though William didn't seem to notice the way she looked at him.

"Yes, well, higher yields for the tenants means higher yields for the earl," William said. "I wouldn't want Rose to think I was doing all that out of the goodness of my heart."

"Don't worry about that, William; I never would have suspected that to be the reason."

"Well, the rest of us here suspect it." Mrs. Wright laughed. "Some of the other things you have done can't have much effect on the amount of rent you receive. Take the school, for example. I don't know of any other parish that has one as fine as the one you had built." Building schools and helping with the harvest? No wonder William's forearms were so much broader now than when he was younger. "Perhaps," Mrs. Wright said, "things worked out for the best in the end."

William had been walking around, looking for Tiger, but he stopped at Mrs. Wright's words. I wondered if his mind had wandered to the same moment mine had. It was hard to be around William and not think about when he'd come to find me the night before he discovered he was to be heir. It was our last night as friends, but at the time, I hadn't known that.

There had been such a commotion in the house that my parents had gone to their rooms early so as not to be in the family's way. We hadn't seen anyone and didn't yet know what the problem was; it was the one and only time the family hadn't shown up for dinner during all of our visits. Instead of hiding in my room like my parents had, I had made my way to our bench in the garden. We had spent hours together in this very spot that year. William would draw, and I would tell him stories. Somehow, I knew he would come find me here.

I heard him coming before I saw him. His steps were slower than they usually were. When he rounded the corner in the path that brought him into view, I waved, but it was as if he didn't see me. I will never forget the look on his face. He looked hollow. The spark in his eyes was gone; it was as if it were only his shell walking toward me. He'd sat silently on the bench a few feet away from me, and that was how we stayed: silent.

The sun slipped lower in the sky. It had gotten chilly, but I didn't want to leave him. I pulled my shawl tighter around my arms. My movement must have roused him somehow because he turned to look at me, and though I knew he had seen me when he'd first sat down, it was as if he had just realized I was there.

"I would like to lie down," he said in a far-off voice.

I started to stand, to give him room on the bench to stretch out, but he reached his hand over to my shoulders and pushed me back down into a sitting position. He then turned and laid his head in my lap. I raised my hands awkwardly, not knowing where to put them. His knees were curled up on his side of the bench, and he faced outward. We were silent again, and when my arms got tired, I slowly rested my right hand on his side and my left on the arm of the bench. He didn't complain, so I relaxed as we watched the sun dip below the horizon. With William's head on my lap, even with the drop in temperature, I didn't feel cold.

"Joseph is gone," he finally said. "He married a Spaniard girl with no connections while he was touring the continent." He paused for a moment, and his words slowly sank in. "Father is going to kill him."

"I don't understand. Did you receive a letter?"

"No, he had the decency to come here and tell us in person. But I am not sure he should have; it has been quite a shock to the whole family."

I couldn't think of a response but was secretly relieved to hear that the problem was with Joseph. So many other scenarios had flashed through my mind throughout the long evening. I started to slowly pat his shoulder. He responded by curling up in a tighter ball, his whole body tense.

"Do you think he will be happy?" I asked.

William relaxed slightly, and I could tell he was thinking. "I think he believes he will be happy. He tried to explain to Mother and Father how much he loves his new wife, but they just couldn't accept it. Maybe if he had at least told them before the marriage . . ." He trailed off.

"It will all work out, somehow," I said.

"No, this is not going to end well. When Joseph left, Father sent James to fetch his rifle." William shuddered slightly. "It was only because of my mother's pleadings that he has decided to wait and pursue Joseph tomorrow. I know that Mother thinks sleeping on it will make my father change his mind, but I don't know."

"Surely your father wouldn't shoot him," I said, trying not to sound horrified but not sure I had succeeded.

"I hope you're right. I feel that you're probably right, but I think he would like to threaten him, to show him who has control, and I worry about what could happen in the heat of the moment." William paused again and adjusted his head more comfortably on my lap. He sighed deeply and then said to me, "I had better get back. Perhaps there is something I could do to help my mother." But instead of getting up to leave, he closed his eyes and just stayed where he was.

It seemed as though all the birds on the estate had begun their nighttime chorale at the same time. With all of autumn's beauty surrounding us, I could see why William was hesitant to return to the tumult of Feldstone Manor. I wished there were some way I could help him, but I knew what was going on was much too serious for me to be helpful in any way. I thought back to my childhood, how whenever I had been ill or overly upset, my older sister Elizabeth would stroke my hair. Starting at my temples and working her way to the back of my head, it was one of the most relaxing feelings, and it almost always calmed me down and made me feel better.

I lifted my left hand from the bench and started to stroke William's hair. My fingers moved back and forth in the patterns I remembered my sister using. He let out a long breath of air, and I finally felt his body relax. After several minutes, his breathing deepened to a steady rhythm.

"William?" I whispered.

"Hmm?" he answered, still completely relaxed.

"Oh, I was just checking to make sure you hadn't fallen asleep."

"No," he said quietly. "As much as an escape to sleep sounds divine, I really had better head back in and see if there is anything I can do to help. Perhaps speak one more time to my father."

"All right," I said, stopping my massage, and then without thinking, I bent down and placed a light kiss on his temple. It was what Elizabeth had always done when she finished. William didn't move for a moment, so I hoped fervently that he hadn't noticed. It had been an extremely light kiss, I told myself. Surely he wouldn't know the difference between the touch of my lips and the touch of my fingers at his temple.

He turned his whole body so that he was facing me and the sky, but he wasn't looking at the sky. The gray color of his eyes was somehow different. He didn't look sleepy at all; he looked intrigued. He obviously knew exactly what I had done.

"Rose?" he said with a quirked eyebrow.

Embarrassed at being caught, I jumped up, which practically dumped William unceremoniously onto the ground. He was athletic enough to save himself from the tumble by swinging quickly to his feet.

"I forgot," I quickly said. "I promised my parents I would retire directly after visiting the gardens. I'd better get back."

"I'll walk with you," he said, but I had already started the trek back to the manor. He followed behind me, saying nothing, for which I was grateful. When we got within a few yards of the house and I was about to go in, he jumped a few steps in front of me and turned around. It startled me enough that I stopped moving.

"Thank you, Rose," he said. "I am sorry that you are here to witness my family at our worst, but I am also selfishly glad you were here to give me comfort." At the word *comfort*, our eyes met, and I could tell we were both thinking of the same thing. My accidental kiss. Perhaps I should explain it to him. *I kissed you as a sister!* I wanted to blurt out, but as we stood there looking at each other, I knew it was a lie. It was as if that unintentional kiss were a gossamer thread that tied us together. It would be easy to remove such an insignificant bond, but I hoped neither of us wanted to. It was ridiculous for me, the fifth daughter of a baronet, to feel any sort of romantic regard for the son of an earl, but as William reached up and tucked a stray lock of hair behind my ear, it seemed a lot less ridiculous.

"Good night, William," I said in a short puff of breath and then turned and ran into the house. It took me hours to fall asleep that night. Something had changed between William and me, and it both excited and scared me.

The next morning at breakfast, everything changed again. Lord Chatsworth had stood up in the middle of the meal and instructed us all to call William Lord Telford from then on. It was the title Joseph had been using. "My son Joseph, if you ever have cause to see or address him again, which I am quite sure you won't, will now just be Mr. Lawrence. I will allow him to keep the family name, but that is all. He shall have no title."

William barely spoke at all during breakfast and never looked me in the eye. For two days, I never had the chance to speak to him alone, and I was dying to know how he was faring amid all the change. When I finally bumped into him in the hall when no one else was around, I grabbed his elbow as he tried to walk right past me.

"William?" I said. I had hoped he would want to confide in me. Instead, he tore his arm out of my grasp and stepped quickly to the side.

"It is Lord Telford now," he said, disdain practically dripping from the words. "We really shouldn't be so familiar with each other now that I am the heir." And then he left me standing there, my young heart unable to completely grasp what his words meant. The thin thread had been snapped, and not gently. It had been torn away, leaving a wound that I feared would never heal.

I called him Lord Telford for two days, and then gave up trying to discover exactly what had happened. Instead, I started agitating him every chance I got, beginning by still using his Christian name. I decided that even though I might not ever be friends with William again, by the heavens, I would not allow him to ignore me.

"Tiger!" Mrs. Wright yelled again, pulling me out of my visit to the past. This time a brown-and-black-striped animal slinked along the house and into the back garden, where we were standing.

"He is huge!" I exclaimed. I focused only on Tiger, not daring to look at William. His all-seeing eyes would certainly know I had been thinking about us.

"It is all the milk you and Lord Telford brought him. That and the mice," Mrs. Wright said. I bent down and stretched my fingers out to him. He slowly walked over and licked them. I laughed in delight at the rough tongue on the inside of my hand.

"I am sorry I brought you no treats," I said. "Not that you need any."

William bent over and handed me a wrapped-up piece of dried bacon. I raised my eyebrow at him but took it, opened it, and gave it to Tiger, who grabbed it and ate it in one large bite.

"I thought we might run into Tiger here," William said.

For someone who had been adamant that we not go inside, he certainly was prepared.

A babe crying inside the home made us all forget Tiger for the moment. Mrs. Wright jumped up to go inside and fetch the child. With nothing else to do outside, we all followed her back into the house. We waited for her in the sitting room. The basket we brought was tipped on its side, the toys were scattered about, and some of the younger children were playing happily with them.

Mrs. Wright came out of the back room carrying a small bundle. "Meet my little one," she said. "Henry."

"He is beautiful," I told her, and she promptly placed him in my arms. Henry's blond little head nestled perfectly in the crook of my arm. He was still very small but old enough to smile back at me as I cooed to him from above. I pressed my nose just under his chin and could smell damp milk. I shook my head back and forth, and he gurgled at my touch. I hadn't been flattering Mrs. Wright; he really was a beautiful child.

William placed his pinky in the child's chubby little hand. Henry grabbed his finger firmly. For an instant, our eyes met and it felt like a spring thaw. I waited for him to look down and pull away from me, and he did, but it took a few heartbeats longer than I'd thought it would.

"Congratulations, Mrs. Wright," William said as he walked away from me and toward her. "You have another healthy son."

"Thank you, Lord Telford. He is a joy already."

I joined the two of them and carefully handed the babe back to his mother.

"And now, unfortunately, we need to get back to the estate," William said. "It has been a pleasure." He placed his hand on my lower back and ushered me toward the door. His touch made me forget my manners, and I nearly forgot to say goodbye. As the door shut behind us, he quickly removed his hand and started at a brisk pace back toward the manor house.

I caught up with him and made the mistake of trying to elicit a conversation out of him. "See? That wasn't so bad. I don't know what all the fuss was about bringing me on this visit."

He stopped and turned, furious. His eyes were such a dark gray they were almost black. "I need you to stay away from me for the rest of this visit. Do you understand?"

I had never seen William so upset, not since Joseph had run off, and I unconsciously took a step back. "I'm sorry, William. I don't know what I did wrong, but—"

"Don't apologize!" he said in frustration. "Just leave me the devil alone for the rest of your time here. That is all I ask. Please." By the end of his lecture, I could feel that his anger had simmered away into something that sounded more like exhaustion. I had no idea why being around me was so tiresome to him.

I closed my lips tightly, worried that I would say something I would regret. To my utter mortification, I felt tears start to well up in my eyes. Instead of giving William the pleasure of seeing how much he had hurt me, I turned on my heel and stomped ahead of him, hoping to leave him far enough behind that he wouldn't catch up.

I was looking down at my skirts as I desperately tried to put distance between us. My breath was turning ragged, and I knew I should probably slow down, but I continued at my reckless pace. I almost passed the apple tree before it registered in the corner of my vision. Once I saw it, though, I quickly turned off the path before I could change my mind. I didn't care what William's reasons were for not wanting me to go there anymore, and I wouldn't stay away just to try to please him.

The tall grasses pulled at my skirts, but I didn't slow, and I didn't try to lift them. I just plowed forward, knowing that William couldn't be too far behind. My pace slowed as I neared the base of the tree. I took a deep breath and, for a moment, heard the memory of laughter on the wind as it caressed my face. William and I had spent many happy afternoons here, and I had never been back since.

I shouldn't be here, I thought. I shouldn't be sullying this place with my anger and resentment. Our apple tree knew only the youngsters who had happily sat in its branches, capturing fruit and daring each other to go higher.

The wind shifted, and my eye caught something on the opposite side of the tree. I stepped into the shade provided by that side and looked closer. Someone had nailed footholds from the lowest parts of the trunk up to some of the highest branches. Whatever William had been worried about before, it must not have been that I would fall again. It would be hard to fall from a tree so painstakingly altered.

I looked back at the pathway to see if William was following me, but he wasn't. He didn't look anywhere except ahead. He didn't give any indication that he had seen me leave the path and head out to the tree, but I knew it would have been impossible for him not to notice. I turned back to the tree, stepped closer, and examined the smooth grain on each small platform. The fourth step up was roughly eye level, and on the lower right-hand side, the delicate shape of a rose had been burnt into the wood. I rubbed my hand over it in confusion, feeling the deep grooves that formed the largest of the petals. I looked back to the path once more for a reaction from William, but he had continued on his way, around a bend, and out of sight.

I reached up and plucked a low-hanging apple from the tree, wiped it slowly on my dress, and took a bite. As the delicious juice from the apple filled my mouth, I studied those wooden planks. There was only one person I could think of who would have placed them there, and he wanted nothing to do with me.

CHAPTER 4

My parents and I sat with the Chatsworth family, minus Lady Chatsworth, in the drawing room, awaiting dinner. I had opted to sit in one of the oversized leather club chairs, even though the men usually sat in them. This one was positioned off by itself, near the bookshelf, so I hoped no one would come try to converse with me. I sank deep into the soft, supple leather and hoped my mother wouldn't take note of my posture.

It had been a week since William and I had visited Mrs. Wright, and I had followed his edict to stay away from him precisely. We had hardly spoken more than a few words to each other and only in the presence of others. Perhaps I should have started out this way and saved myself from the pain. Just because we were currently living in the same house didn't mean we had to interact, did it? I had seen his mother on a few occasions, but each time, she had seemed worse. When I'd seen her yesterday, she hadn't allowed me to open the drapes at all.

I wondered what was taking the staff so long to prepare dinner. I thought I had arrived in the drawing room at the last minute, as I was hoping to avoid as much contact with William as possible. My toe tapped a nervous rhythm inside my slipper; it must be time to go in and eat. The main door opened, and Lady Chatsworth entered, looking better than she had for days, perhaps even years. Her hair was styled meticulously with ringlets on each side of her head. Her dress was fresh, as if it had never been worn. But the biggest difference was in her eyes. They sparkled with a fervent energetic light. She smiled at all of us and turned to Howard, the butler, and told him that now that she was here, they could announce dinner.

William immediately stood, walked over to his mother, and gave her a hearty kiss on the cheek. "Mother, it is wonderful to see you looking so well!"

"William!" she replied, giving his shoulder a soft push. "We all know it is because of you I am feeling so much better in body and in spirit."

Lord Chatsworth laughed deeply at his wife's comment. He seemed well aware of what was going on. My parents looked as surprised as I did, so apparently I wasn't the only one who didn't know what exactly William had done to invigorate his mother so much. I wished that whatever it was, I would have thought of it first. Lady Chatsworth looked as if she had been cured from years of ill health.

I followed my mother into the dining room, but it felt different this time with Lady Chatsworth leading us in. It felt complete and as it should have been all along. I couldn't help smiling as I sat down. I looked across the table to William, but he wouldn't meet my eye. That was nothing new. Had I hoped that with his mother feeling better perhaps he would warm up to me again? It was silly. Somehow my smile was not quite as broad as I turned my attention to dinner.

"William," Lady Chatsworth began after everyone had helped themselves to some sustenance. "Have you given any thought to where you would like to have the wedding? It will be quite cold soon, so perhaps London would be a wiser location than the chapel here."

The venison in my mouth suddenly became dry and hard to chew. William's eyes flashed to my own and then quickly to his mother's. "No, Mother, I haven't thought through the details. It is all still rather new."

"Lord Telford! You are engaged?" I was grateful that my mother could ask the question. I was still chewing that blasted piece of meat, or at least I started chewing it again after reminding myself it was still there, but it was so dry there was no way I would be able to swallow it anytime soon.

William smiled his wan, pleasant smile that he saved for company. "No, I am afraid not, but I should be soon."

I hadn't heard any rumors about William courting anyone. I didn't follow him closely in society, but I would have heard if he had pursued someone last season. There had been no female visitors in the two weeks we had been here. Whoever this lady was, she had remained quite hidden. Maybe she was horribly disfigured or cruel as a hungry war chief. Poor William—he was extremely rude, but even he didn't deserve cruelty.

"William has promised me that he will marry within a six month. I fear he thinks my health is more dire than it is." Lady Chatsworth paused as if waiting for someone to contradict her, but everyone was silent. With a small laugh, she continued. "Well, at any rate, his promise has given me a renewal of energy."

"But what of a bride?" I asked, shoving the hunk of dry flesh to the side of my mouth.

"Oh," Lady Chatsworth said with a flick of her wrist, "I am not worried about that. Any woman would be ecstatic to marry William." His mother beamed at him, and I was reminded again how much better she looked. "His title and good looks would draw in any woman, and his gentleness will keep her."

His gentleness? It was not quite how I would describe William, not for the past two years anyway. I dared a glance at him. He sat there looking slightly pained but, honestly, still handsome. I noticed how well his arms filled out his shirt coat, the way his throat flexed as he swallowed. His sandy-blond hair had a wave to it that I supposed most women would find hard to resist running their fingers through. And with a title to assume, I realized with a shock that Lady Chatsworth was right. Almost any woman would be ecstatic to make that kind of match. He wouldn't even need the full six months to find a willing bride.

"I don't know if I will be well enough for a whole season, but I will make it for the first few balls, at least," Lady Chatsworth said.

"It has been so long since I have ventured out. I don't even know which eligible ladies are available this year." She spoke as if picking a wife for her son was going to be as easy and convenient as picking which roast to buy from the butcher. *She might not be wrong.*

"We will be there all season and can help Lord Chatsworth with anything necessary. I have managed to marry off four daughters, after all. Not much to it," my mother said, pushing up the curls on the side of her head. "Although Rose does seem to be dragging her feet." I looked up in astonishment that the conversation had turned to me. Weren't we discussing William's prospects? Our eyes met from across the table. Gone was the pained look and his worn-out company smile. His eyes were suddenly alive with interest.

"I have no doubt Miss Davenport's beauty has captured the hearts of many men," Lady Chatsworth said. I couldn't hold William's gaze any longer and, instead, turned my attention to the fine embroidery on the Chatsworth napkins. Two mothers discussing marriage—this conversation might never end!

"Rose's beauty is completely wasted on her." My mother laughed. "She might be of marriageable age, but she shows no signs of interest in marriage. Why, just last season, I was quite certain the Marquis of Blakeley was showing a significant attachment to her, but as soon as I mentioned it to Rose, she suddenly started refusing him dances." My mother showed her exasperation with my behavior by throwing her hands in the air. "I am convinced she is bound and determined to live off of her parents' charity for the rest of her life."

The heat in my face was a sudden fire, but I couldn't find fault in what my mother had said. I had enjoyed spending time with the marquis but had assumed he wasn't interested in furthering a relationship, and while I was still quite sure he wasn't, Mother had been so certain of an attachment that I had no longer been comfortable in his company.

"Lord Blakeley." The earl puffed his name. "I know him well—capital fellow. Not up to snuff for you, Miss Davenport?" I buried my face in my hands. I didn't want to be discussing my prospects in front of my own family, let alone in front of William's.

"You are making poor Rose uncomfortable," William said quietly from across the table.

"Are we truly making you feel uncomfortable?" Lady Chatsworth asked. I pulled my hands away from my face, and she took one look at me and must have realized William was right. She deftly turned the conversation to another topic, and I finally gave up on chewing my venison and just swallowed it whole.

"How would you like your hair dressed this evening?" Lydia asked the same question every night, and even though there were to be guests, I couldn't make myself care much today. It had been a week since William's announcement, and during that time, I had seen him only at mealtimes. Lady Chatsworth was hosting her first dinner party in months, and the house was as busy as a spinning top as everyone readied it for the evening. For me, everything just felt dizzying and hollow.

"Arrange it however you feel would be best, or better yet, arrange it in whatever way is quickest, and then you can have a bit of free time tonight," I told her.

"Dressing your hair really is a pleasure," she told me. "There is hardly a need for my skills except when your family visits."

"That is sweet of you to say, Lydia, but I am certain the pleasure has worn off by now."

"Perhaps a simple braid, then, and I'll wrap it on top of your head. It won't be as lovely as most of the arrangements I have done for you though."

"Perfect," I said.

I tried not to second-guess my decision to dress plainly as my family, the Chatsworth family, and the Rowley family sat down to dinner. I had never met the Rowley family, but they seemed pleasant enough. Mr. and Mrs. Rowley owned a country house and small farm a few miles from Feldstone, and I could tell they had visited often in the past. They had brought their youngest daughter, who must have been a year or two younger than I was. She was blonde and pretty, with a cute button nose dotted with a smattering of freckles.

"Lord Chatsworth," Mr. Rowley started out the conversation at dinner after all the introductions were over. "It is wonderful to be here at Feldstone Manor. It is always an honor to be invited."

Lord Chatsworth returned the pleasantries, and I turned my attention to the white bean soup. I had gotten much better at not goading William, or talking in general, since his to-be engagement was announced. I made it through most of dinner without having to say more than a few words in polite response to questions asked, mostly about life in London. The only person who managed to speak less was Miss Rowley, who, after her initial "Nice to meet you," had not uttered a word. Nor had she taken her eyes off of William. I sighed and took another sip of my wine. It was nice to no longer be in awe of the Chatsworth good looks.

"I noticed the roses in the front have been removed," I heard Mrs. Rowley mention to Lady Chatsworth. I sat straighter in my chair; my soup was no longer quite so interesting. "It is a pity; they were some of the finest in the county."

Yes, they were.

Mr. Rowley furrowed his brows and gave his wife a sharp look. She looked immediately regretful about her choice of words, obviously not wanting to question the decisions of an earl and his family. "But the lions that replaced them are quite handsome, indeed," she said.

"Yes, quite handsome, indeed," her husband added. "I have never seen such ferocious-looking lions."

Lady Chatsworth laughed, and I saw William's eyes widen. He gave his mother a small shake of his head. Perhaps he didn't want her to tell everyone at the table that he had removed the roses to spite me.

"They started to die off," Lady Chatsworth said without acknowledging William's look. "We never could discover the reason why. Heaven knows, William tried like the devil to save them."

"Mother!" William cried louder than necessary for such a small gathering. Every head turned to look at William. After a moment's pause, he quietly added, "Your language."

"Oh, hush, William. I only say it because it is true." She turned back to Mrs. Rowley. "He had specialists from all over looking at them." William's head drooped down, and he took a deep breath. "The bushes were all but dead and looking terrible, and still, he wouldn't allow the gardener to pull them. I don't know what possessed him to care so much about those particular roses, but he wouldn't give up."

William groaned slightly. My spoon had paused in midair at some point. I couldn't remember when. I quickly put it back into my bowl, even though I hadn't yet eaten the soup from it.

"I was feeling ill at the time," Lady Chatsworth said. "But almost every evening, Reginald would give me a report of some new remedy William had tried. It was the most diverting thing to happen all summer."

"I tried to have those brown, decaying bushes removed multiple times," Lord Chatsworth piped up with a chuckle. "He always had one last thing he wanted to try."

"Reginald finally pulled them up and installed the lions right over their place while William was on a trip to London," Lady Chatsworth said. "If it weren't for those lions, we would probably still have dead rosebushes at our entrance." She laughed again, and the sound rippled through the room until it faded. "Such a strange episode."

"Well, they were lovely blooms," Mrs. Rowley said to William, who was still looking at his soup. "I think it was right of you to try to save them."

"But also right of you to cover them, Lord Chatsworth," her husband quickly added, glancing worriedly between father and son. "Correct of both of you, for sure."

My mind was spinning so quickly, not even Mr. Rowley's logic fazed me. William had tried to save the roses. I waited for an explanation from William, or even a look, but he had gone back to eating and kept his head down.

After dinner, the men stayed in the dining room for a smoke. On our way to the drawing room, I had a hard time keeping up with the conversation among the ladies. I did catch that Lady Chatsworth declared that we should play whist when the men returned.

"Oh, quite right!" Mrs. Rowley said. "Whist will be just the thing!"

Lady Chatsworth decided that I should be on her team. "I remember you being quite good with cards even at a young age. I don't think anyone will have a chance against us."

"I won't be playing this evening," my mother said. "You will have to get one of the men to play on your team, Mrs. Rowley."

"Mr. Rowley always enjoys a rousing game of whist, unless, of course, the earl would like to play; in which case, either he or I would be honored to sit out with Lady Davenport," Mrs. Rowley said, giving my mother a smile that I assumed was supposed to be endearing.

"What of Miss Rowley? Will you be playing this evening?" I asked. Perhaps if she wanted to join in, I could be excused.

Miss Rowley's face flushed a shade darker, and she shook her head, her blonde curls bouncing with innocent shyness.

"Jane plays rather well," her mother explained, "but playing among such illustrious company as this evening's would be quite taxing for her, I am afraid."

Mrs. Rowley glanced back and forth between Lady Chatsworth and the door. "I suppose we'll just have to see what the men want when they return." She began fidgeting with her dress, smoothing the skirt and pulling at her sleeves.

When the men returned, minus William, I noted, as did Miss Rowley, Mrs. Rowley quickly piped up before anyone else could say anything. "Mr. Rowley, Lady Chatsworth would like to play whist. She has requested Miss Davenport to be her partner. So it just remains to be seen who will be on the other team."

"Oh," Mr. Rowley said. He looked back and forth between Lord Chatsworth and my father. "Whist sounds delightful. What a capital idea. Lord Chatsworth, will you be playing?"

"Heavens, no. I'll let the ladies enjoy their card game."

"I'm out as well," my father said. "Whist was never my strong point."

"Quite right, quite right. We shall let the ladies play, then," Mr. Rowley said while looking longingly at the card table.

"But Mama and Miss Rowley will not be playing, Mr. Rowley," I said. "So I suppose, if you are not against it, we would be much obliged if you would join us." Someone needed to put the man out of his misery, and at this point, I just wanted the game over as quickly as possible.

"Oh," Mr. Rowley said as his face lit up. "If I'm needed, then I'm happy to assist you in this manner, Lady Chatsworth."

"Thank you, Mr. Rowley. You will be on Mrs. Rowley's team. I hope that is not too disagreeable?"

"No, of course not. Whatever you feel is best, for certain."

Lady Chatsworth was sorely disappointed in my card-playing skills. Although normally quite acute at cards, I was too distracted to follow what was happening during each trick. It was almost as painful watching her disappointment as it was watching the worry on the Rowleys' faces as they realized they were winning. I tried to make myself care a bit more, but for the life of me, I could not. I wanted only to finish out the evening so I could be alone and think more clearly about what had been said at dinner. As I played my final card, Lady Chatsworth's shoulders slumped. Mr. and Mrs. Rowley exchanged desperate glances, and Mrs. Rowley reluctantly played a higher card than mine. I didn't have to wait to see what Lady Chatsworth played to know the Rowleys had won the trick and the whole game in only one set.

CHAPTER 5

"COULD YOU LIFT YOUR ARM, miss?" Lydia asked later that evening. She gave me a funny look through my vanity mirror; this must not have been the first time she had asked. I quickly lifted my arm. I was having a hard time hearing her as she asked me to turn this way or that so she could get me out of my gown. My thoughts were much too loud.

After Lydia left, I climbed into bed and stared at the ceiling instead of sleeping. Although my body was tired, my mind felt more awake than it had been for days, and it would not let me rest. I tried to picture William bringing in specialists to save my roses, but I couldn't. It was completely incongruent with his actions toward me. I rolled onto my side and punched my pillow. Hours passed this way until, in the stillness of the night, I threw away my inhibitions and, at the first hazy sign of dawn, got out of bed and helped myself into my dressing gown.

I knew William would avoid me today; we would see each other only in company. We wouldn't have a chance to actually speak. I quickly penned a note to him and then slowly turned the handle on my door and peeked into the hallway. I knew the servants would be downstairs, awake and moving throughout the house, but they wouldn't be likely to disturb family or guests for at least another hour.

I made my way to William's chamber, lack of sleep making me reckless. The corridor that led to the family wing was long, seemingly much longer than it had been when I'd made my way to see Lady Chatsworth. I was sure I would be caught, but my initial assessment must have been correct; the servants were all still downstairs. I should have turned around and gone back to my room, but I couldn't. An idea had been flowing through my mind all night, and I wouldn't be able to rest until I knew if what I suspected was correct.

Perhaps William didn't hate me after all.

When I arrived at his door, I stood there for a moment, tracing a knot in the grain of the wood with my finger. The smell of baking bread wafted all the way up from the kitchens and into the empty hallway, reminding me I wasn't alone in the house. I didn't dare knock, but I couldn't wait outside either. More than likely, a servant would come into his room before he ever left it. I bent down to push the note under the door before I could rethink my decision.

The door opened before the note even touched the floor, and someone walked right into me, toppling me to the ground. I bit my lip to prevent any noise as I fell, but it did me little good, for the man was not so careful.

"What the devil!" William exclaimed from above me. His leg was tangled in the skirt of my nightdress, and I could smell sandalwood in the air. Grateful it was William and not a servant, I righted myself to a sitting position, pulled my skirts free, and quickly shushed him.

"Rose," he whispered, kneeling down to look at me in horror. "What are you doing here?"

His hair was mussed and his shirt open at the top, with no cravat. It looked like he had hastily tucked his shirt into his breeches. Because of his crouched position and the looseness of the fabric, I could see partway down his shirt to the smooth skin that covered his chest. I swallowed hard and tried to remember what the question was he had asked me. Shaking my head slightly, I jerked my eyes to his face, but I was still unable to voice my plan. I just held out my note, both hands reaching up to him like a supplication.

He didn't take it but grabbed both my hands and helped me up to a standing position. The darkness of the early-morning in the hallway seemed suddenly dangerous. We were inches apart, and his hands were still holding mine. If anyone were to discover us here, it would be disastrous.

"Is anything wrong?" he asked, his eyes darting back and forth between my own. "My mother . . ."

"Your mother is fine," I said. "As far as I know, anyway."

"Your parents? Do you need something from me?" My eyes drifted to his collarbone, still exposed, even though he was now standing. I was sure rainwater could pool in the hollows behind that collarbone. I suddenly felt the urge to run my fingertips along the ridge of it. Was his skin as smooth as it looked?

"Rose . . ."

I shifted my gaze back to his eyes. They were dark and unreadable, but the idea that he might be able to read my thoughts made me want to look away.

"You look as scared as Tiger was when we first found him near the Wrights' home. Please tell me what is going on."

His hands were still cradling mine lightly. He was my old William, the one who used to care about me and show it.

"My parents are fine," I said. He hadn't taken my note. I felt incapable of explaining my reasons for coming. I kept my eyes locked on his as I slid my hands out of his grasp, tucked the note into my sash and then ran my fingers slowly up his arms. I needed a reminder that he was no longer the young boy I used to know. It was a good reminder. With my hands at the top of his broad shoulders, my fingertips were only inches away from the right temple I had kissed so long ago. I reached up and touched it gently.

"If you aren't going to tell me what is wrong, you need to leave," William said. "Now." But he didn't back away. His eyes were closed as if he was in some kind of pain. And I hoped it was the same kind of ache I was feeling. "Please."

I agreed with him. Of course I agreed with him. But after a night of no sleep and with my question still burning, I swallowed the fear that had kept me from explaining myself and decided not to wait until he would meet me in the garden this afternoon as my note had requested. Truthfully, I doubted that plan would have worked anyway. I had him alone now. I took my hand off of his face and let my fingers glide slowly back down his arms, enjoying every ridge of hardness in ways that I probably had no right to. When I reached his hands, which were closed tightly, I opened them and placed my palms back inside his.

"Do you hate me, William?" I asked quietly, not daring to look up at him. Instead, my eyes looked once again at his powerful collarbone. It might not have been the most appropriate place to fasten my eyes, but they were drawn there anyway. I could see his pulse just above it. I was no doctor, but it seemed to be racing. It took him a moment to respond, and to distract myself from the fear of his answer, I counted his pulse.

"Do I hate you?" William whispered finally. "That is why you are here? To ask me if I hate you?" I could hear the incredulity in his voice.

I gathered my courage and looked up at him then, knowing my heart must be in my eyes. As our gazes met, I bit my lip in hesitation. William must be able to see the second half of my question; if he didn't hate me, was there any chance he might care for me?

I heard a sharp intake of breath from him. He dropped my hands as if they had suddenly become unbearably hot and stepped back, away from me. He ran both of his hands through his unkempt hair. "No, Rose," he said softly after a moment's pause. "I don't hate you." He looked up and down the hallway. "Now, please leave; this isn't safe."

"I will leave," I said, taking a small step toward William. He seemed to grow taller as he pressed himself against the doorway. "But first, please tell me if you were the one who placed the footholds on our apple tree." He didn't answer, but his eyes stayed on mine. "If you won't answer me that question, then tell me why you tried to save the roses. And why didn't you tell me you tried to save the roses?" Again, he was silent; the only sound in the hallway was that of our shared breathing. "Why are you determined to have me think the worst of you?"

The left side of his mouth curled up, and his shoulders relaxed. "If I was determined to have you think the worst of me"—his eyes flashed to my lips momentarily—"I could think of a few things I could do right now." His lips were still stuck in a half smile, only a sliver of white showing beneath them. It was not the smirk that he had been giving me for the last two years, nor was it his sincere smile of friendship. This smile was different, darker; it hid secrets I wanted to uncover.

"What things?" I asked. My voice was low, a whisper that held an unspoken dare. My poor night's sleep must have removed all rational thinking from my mind. My eyes traveled up from his mouth, taking in his appearance once again. He hadn't shaved recently, and pale stubble covered his cheeks. His hair was tousled as if he had been running his hands through it repeatedly. As he studied my lips and then the length of my long braid, a wild look flashed in his eyes. I ran my hand down my hair to smooth it. It must look completely disheveled. His eyes seemed to grow darker. He looked like some of the ruffians I had seen on the few occasions I had been near the docks: wild, unpredictable men who had no use for society or its rules.

I hoped he felt like he looked.

"Things"—he bent so that his face was nearer mine. His hand cupped my face, and his thumb stroked my cheekbone. With his other hand, he lightly touched a tendril of hair that had escaped my braid. *Finally*, I thought. I had taken complete liberties with him, touching his arms and temple. It was high time he returned the favor—"that would be extremely inappropriate for the son of an earl to do with the fifth daughter of a baronet." He stood abruptly and moved to the side to create space between us. "So leave, Miss Davenport, before we both regret that you came here so alone and unprotected."

My head jerked away from him. His speech was a knife to my heart. I couldn't move as I processed what he had said. He turned to leave on whatever errand I had interrupted. A piece of my heart seemed to break off and leave with him. I had already humiliated myself, and I was tired of pretending to dislike him. With my heart in my throat, I decided to ask one more thing of him. "I miss us," I said. "I won't ask for anything more; you've made it very clear how inappropriate that would be. But do you ever wonder if we could go back to the way we were before?" His steps paused, and he turned his ear slightly toward me. Knowing I had his attention, I continued. "I loved you as a brother." He turned back to look at me with a smile that didn't reach his eyes.

"I know you did, and that is exactly why we can never go back. I will never love you as a sister." He sounded hollow as he said it, devoid of all the emotions I had felt from him earlier.

I stepped farther away from him and grabbed the collar of my dressing gown, pulling it tighter around my neck as if it could protect me from his words. I pressed my lips together in an effort to hide my hurt. William seemed to soften slightly at the sight of my distress. I knew him well enough to know that he never liked to injure anyone, even me. My habitual mask of indifference and disdain must have melted away, leaving only an image of raw pain in its place. I turned to flee. I couldn't handle his kindness; it would break me more than his harsh words had. Before I could even take my first step away from him, he grasped the tips of my fingers lightly and held me there.

"I'm sorry, Rose," he said as if I were a small child who needed to be handled carefully. "What was in your note?"

I shook my head and pulled my hand out of his. "It was nothing," I replied, not daring to face him.

"You came to my bedchamber practically in the nighttime over a note that was nothing?" he asked. "That doesn't seem very likely."

He might have assumed my note had been more than it was, so I just handed it to him. He took it from me and read it slowly before responding.

"I am sorry. I won't be able to meet you in the garden this afternoon," he said in a monotone that belied emotion. "I am leaving for London this morning. I awoke early to prepare."

"Oh," was my barely audible reply.

"I know what my mother said about the roses, and perhaps there were other things that could have given you cause to think I might hold you in some special regard, but, Rose, I should have probably just said this a long time ago. There can be nothing for us in the future. It is impossible. I think it best to just tell you that now. If I had any inkling that you might have cared for me"—he cleared his throat—"I would have said something before now. I am not trying to push feelings on you that you most likely don't have. I know I have been a brute these past few years, and I would be in shock if you felt any regard for me, but just in case . . . on the off chance you held any tender feelings for me . . ." He paused to take a breath, maybe for me to refute what he said, but I couldn't bring myself to say anything. "I just thought you should know. As long as that is clear, I'll try to be kinder in the future."

"Thank you," I replied ridiculously, and then I fled. This time he didn't try to stop me.

He doesn't hate me, I told myself as I walked furiously down the hallway. That was what I had wanted to ask, and I had gotten my answer. *He doesn't hate me.* I repeated the phrase over and over until I reached my room. I opened the door softly and then closed it behind me. I dropped my dressing gown onto the floor and crawled into bed.

But he doesn't care for me either.

He might find me attractive. He must. My fingers went unwillingly to my lips, where William's gaze had settled just moments ago. But he couldn't love me or have any remote interest in me. With only six months to find a bride, I knew that a daughter of a baronet wouldn't be such a scandalous match. Disadvantageous, perhaps, but matches like that were made every day. I was no unknown Spaniard. If he had felt for me what I had allowed myself to hope in the audacious wee hours of the morning, it would be easy to overcome that difference. No, William didn't hate me. He didn't care enough to hate me or love me, and I felt a fool for believing he might.

William was indifferent.

I don't know why I was so surprised or hurt by the revelation; I was used to such emotions. My own mother cared more for her little pug than she did for me. I closed my eyes, feeling foolish for not having slept all night. Exhaustion settled over me like a heavy blanket. If I was fortunate, I could sleep for an hour or two before Lydia roused me to dress for breakfast.

It seemed as though I had only just drifted off when I was awakened by a small piece of paper being slipped under my bedroom door. The fact that the light ruffle of paper and the footsteps that faded after had awoken me was a testament to how fitfully I had been sleeping. Curiosity piqued, I pulled the heavy down blanket off of me and walked on the cold stone floor over to the doorway. I picked up the small slip of paper. It had been torn from a sketchbook, and even in the dim light, I recognized the bold thick strokes that somehow managed to portray a delicate flower. It was a rose, and it was from William. I was completely awake now, my body a rush of emotions. I darted to the window, cold floors forgotten. I needed more light in order to read the note scribbled hastily under the rose.

Thank you for our first year. Sorry about the last two.
—W

My heart sank as I absentmindedly released the paper and it dropped to the floor. It was only a note to say goodbye.

CHAPTER 6

London

I CHECKED MYSELF IN THE mirror. It was immensely relieving to be back in my own bedroom in London after the disastrous last two weeks of our Feldstone visit. After William left, Lord and Lady Chatsworth continued to host us with perfect hospitality, but following my early-morning confrontation with William, it was a strain to remain in his home. He wrote to his mother often, and although she never read any portion of his letters aloud, I knew he must be keeping her apprised of his search for a suitable bride. Otherwise, I was quite certain she would have returned to her melancholy state and remained in her bedroom once again.

By the time we finally left, I had begun to hate Feldstone. There were no roses on the rosebushes any longer. The hallways were empty and quiet. I had come to one very solid conclusion: I couldn't watch William build a family here, even if it meant his mother regained her health. I would not join my family in another hunting visit and submit myself to the humiliation of watching William with a new bride. It was time I got serious about finding a husband myself. William would be married before the end of the season, and I was bound and determined that I would be too or, at the very least, that I would be married before next Michaelmas.

We had arrived in London a week ago, but tonight was the first ball of the season. Johanna was not quite the master Lydia was with my hair, but she had done her best, and with my new gown for the new season, I felt confident in my ability to turn heads. My dress had arrived just yesterday and was a brilliant emerald green, with a square neck and full short sleeves. I knew I would stand out in a sea of whites and golds. Jewel colors were no longer popular with the women, but I knew the men didn't care a fig about what colors were "in" for the season. I was not going to the Wilmington's ball to impress the women.

I fastened my emerald earrings, pinched my cheeks, and stood tall. My father was only a baronet, and my dowry was just a fifth portion of a third portion of a small inheritance left to my mother and her two other sisters. Nevertheless, I had seen how the men looked at me during the last two seasons. I knew that some things trumped station in life, and for a large portion of men, beauty was one of them. I was going to capture an earl or higher. I would never leave William in doubt of whether or not I regretted not being able to catch his eye.

I descended the stairs, and my mother and father looked appreciative of the time I had spent on my preparations.

"Don't worry, Mother. I am not planning on living off of your charity for the rest of my life. I will catch myself a husband this season—perhaps tonight."

"Well, you certainly look capable of it in that gown," my father said.

"You do look stunning," Mother agreed. "But I really don't know that emerald is quite the right color for the season." Her eyes darted to the stairs as if deciding whether or not it was worth it to have me return and find something more suitable to wear.

"But it is the perfect color for our Rose," my father said. "No man will be able to resist her charms tonight."

I smiled warmly at my father and hoped he was right.

Unfortunately, my father was right, at least as far as Lord Humphreys was concerned. I had managed to dance with the ridiculous man only one time, but I could see that he was headed my way once again. It just so happened that the next dance on my dance card was the only one I hadn't managed to fill. I rubbed my hand self-consciously. There was still a stain on my glove from his last wet kiss, and I desperately wanted to avoid another one. As a marquis, his rank was higher than William's, but I highly doubted anyone would consider him a better match. At nearly forty, he had lost most of his hair and eaten more than he should have, and he sprayed slightly whenever he pronounced any word that started with the letter *f.*

I looked frantically around the room, careful not to meet Lord Humphreys's eye. The Wilmington's ball was the first of the season, and it was always an absolute crush. All along the periphery of the ballroom, there were scores of lords and ladies conversing, which left me nowhere to hide. The refreshment room, adjacent and open to the ballroom, where I was currently standing, was the same. The buffet table, heavy with decadent pastries and fruit dishes, was no help either, unless I wanted to duck under it—which I desparately wanted to—but I decided against it.

I meandered away from the table and back into the ballroom, weaving in and out of guests until I came to the french doors that led out to the balcony and, from there, to the garden. The chilly autumn evening air would keep most of the guests inside. Perhaps in the garden I could find a place to free myself from Lord Humphreys. I had almost reached the large, open doorway leading out to the balcony when I realized my mistake. Being caught by Lord Humphreys in the garden would be much worse than being caught in the ballroom, even if it did mean another damp glove.

I caught a hurried glimpse of my harasser only to find, to my surprise, that he had been waylaid by a blessed army colonel! If I found a place to secret myself while he was occupied, perhaps he would think I *had* gone to the garden and would search for me there. With nowhere to hide inside the massive ballroom, I inspected the balcony once again. It was a large stone balcony, open to the garden below. Several columns reached high up to the third floor, where there was a higher balcony. I considered taking the stairs up to it, but I didn't want to be rude. I wasn't aware if guests were welcomed there.

Finally, I saw what could be my only option. Flanking each side of the doorway just outside the ballroom were two large potted evergreen trees. They were conical and dense enough that I couldn't see behind them. Perfect for hiding behind but close enough to allow me a quick return inside if I were unfortunate enough to be found. The only disadvantage was that they were flanked on the outside by the balcony's balustrade. I would have only one escape route from the hiding place—back the way I had come.

Before I lost my nerve, I backed slowly behind the closest one, keeping a careful eye on the doorway to the ballroom. It wouldn't be seemly to be seen hiding at a ball. When I was finally completely out of view and behind the potted tree, I was happy to note that I could still see some parts of the ballroom through the branches. I should at least have some warning if anyone were to come, even though I was quite certain no one would see me. At last, confident I was safe, I breathed a heavy sigh of relief.

"I hope you never had cause to hide from me like this last season," a distinctly masculine voice behind me said. My hands flew to my throat, and I spun around. There, in the cramped space between the potted tree and the outside balustrade was the Marquis of Blakeley.

"Lord Blakeley!" I exclaimed, starting to back up so I could leave him to the hiding place he had found first. He stood straight and tall and looked over my head. The space seemed to shrink with his nearness.

"I wouldn't do that if I were you," he warned. "Lord Humphreys is headed this way."

I immediately stopped. Lord Blakeley behind a pot was better than Lord Humphreys on a balcony any day. "Was I that obvious?" I whispered.

"Maybe to others you were not, but my eye has been fixed on you for a good portion of the evening." He sighed. "Do you avoid all men so arduously or just marquises?"

"I am quite certain I never resorted to actually hiding from you, Lord Blakeley, but I may have to after this debacle." There was not much room in our hiding spot, and Lord Blakeley seemed to take up most of it. His dark hair had enough curl in it to make him seem an inch taller than he was, not that he needed the height. I once again tried to shift backward to give him more room, but he shook his head and put a finger up to his lips. Was there someone there behind me? I longed to turn and look, but I was worried the movement would alert them to where we were hiding.

"I hope you won't start hiding from me," Lord Blakeley whispered after a moment of silence, leaning forward so he would not be heard by anyone nearby. "Well, not unless I am concealing myself in the location first, anyway. Hiding together has its advantages."

"Advantages?" I asked. He was close enough that I could see specks of gold in his brown eyes.

"Yes, advantages," he repeated while raising one thick eyebrow. "I can keep an eye out for your unwanted marquis, and you would be the first one discovered if anyone actually did find us. No one would think two people could fit here."

I gave him my best glare, but he just grinned boyishly back at me. At least I knew he was jesting. It was hard to be angry at someone with a dimple. "You're despicable," I said like a true coquette.

"I must admit," he said, bending closer to me and lowering his voice enough that I couldn't help but lean toward him, "I was hoping you wouldn't be quite so ravishing this year. You have disappointed me completely in that regard."

The space seemed to grow even smaller. Uncomfortable with the topic of conversation, I decided to change it. "You have discovered who I am running from, but I have not yet heard your explanation for hiding behind this monstrous creation."

"Me? Hiding?" he scoffed. "I am just inexplicably fond of plants," he said with that innocent smile, and I held back a laugh as I wondered why I had ignored Lord Blakeley for the final part of last season. He was quite pleasant.

"I am sorry I snubbed you last year," I said spontaneously. "I was enjoying our time together, but . . ."

"I became too attached?" Lord Blakeley finished for me.

"My mother seemed to think so," I quickly defended myself. "I never did; truly, I didn't."

"I have always liked your mother. She is quite astute," he said, stepping closer to me until we were only inches apart. He reached one arm slowly toward me. I closed my eyes and turned my head away from him. He chuckled, a low pleasant sound that was distinctly mocking. My eyes flew open only to see that he had reached up behind me to move away some of the branches in order to get a better view. "The way is clear," he said. "Perhaps we could continue this conversation in a more appropriate setting." He paused. "Like a dance? That is, unless you are planning once again to snub me this season."

"No," I replied, and his face fell. I quickly clarified, "I meant to say, no, I am not planning on snubbing you this season, and I would love to dance." I smiled up at him, and his dimple returned. I happily turned around to face the ballroom again. With Lord Blakeley at my side, Lord Humphreys no longer felt like much of a threat.

As Lord Blakeley led me back into the crowd, I scanned the room, not for the first time, for William. As far as I could tell, he wasn't here. My sister Elizabeth noticed me with Lord Blakeley and raised an eyebrow. She had witnessed my complete avoidance of him at the end of last season and must have been wondering what exactly had changed. I gave her a smile of reassurance. I was only too happy to oblige Lord Blakeley this time around.

We performed our bows and curtsies, and then the two couples next to us started off the quadrille. Even though it was unnecessary, I took Lord Blakeley by the arm as we watched them perform the first round of the set. His eyes widened at my touch, and he then reached across his front and placed his hand on mine.

"I am quite enjoying not being snubbed, Miss Davenport. I hope to remain in your good graces for the remainder of the season," Lord Blakeley said. His insecurity seemed to make him even more handsome.

"I hope so as well, although the fickleness of women is well documented by poets and playwrights. This is only the first ball of the season. Who knows how I will feel about you two weeks from now." I would hate for him to be too confident, even though I was sure he would be equally good-looking in that case.

"Well then, I shall make it a point to enjoy every moment that I do meet with your approval," he said just before we made our way to the center of the circle. I was aware of every light touch to my back and every touch of our gloved hands as we made the twist and turns of the quadrille. But by far, my favorite thing about dancing with Lord Blakeley was that when I smiled at him, he smiled back.

"Would you like any refreshment?" he asked after we took our final bow.

"I really would rather join my sister Elizabeth until the next dance begins."

"I'll escort you to her," he said. Once again, I was led through the crushing crowd, with the marquis's hand at my back.

We reached Elizabeth, and I thanked Lord Blakeley for the dance.

"I have been anticipating a dance with you for the better part of a year. The pleasure was all mine." He gave Elizabeth and me a small bow. He then left us and was soon lost in the crowd.

"Lord Blakeley?" Elizabeth asked with a sly smile.

"Lord Blakeley," I replied with a nod, feeling self-satisfied.

"I thought last year you cast him aside," she whispered to me.

"Yes, I suppose I did, but this year I feel differently."

"Well, I hope you know how you feel, because I am quite certain his feelings for you are significant." A tiny prick of doubt touched my heart at her words, for in truth, I wasn't sure how I felt about Lord Blakeley, but I knew I enjoyed his company. And even more than that, I was certain he enjoyed mine. It was a position I could appreciate being in.

The rest of the ball went by in a whirlwind, and I had to admit it was nice to be back in London with more for entertainment and company than Lord Chatsworth's family. William never showed, which I thought was rather odd, seeing as he was in a rush to find a fiancée. Overall, it was a huge relief that I didn't have to see him.

CHAPTER 7

My mother and I sat across from each other at the small round table in our breakfast room. The window across from us was situated to let the bright sun shine into the room on clear mornings, and today was a particularly sunny day. After a late night at the ball, the brightness felt jarring instead of cheerful. More than that, the linens on the table and the upholstery on the chairs looked more faded in the harsh light. We didn't entertain many guests in the small room, so it was always the last to receive improvements.

"Flowers for you, miss," the maid said, entering the room, holding a large bouquet of yellow roses. "They are from Lord Blakeley, Marquis of Blakeley." I smiled at the flowers he had sent. It might have been shameless to love them so much, seeing as they were my namesake, but I couldn't help it. I was glad he had chosen to send roses.

"Lord Blakeley!" my mother exclaimed as she eyed me in surprise. Apparently she had missed seeing us dance. "Open the card. Let's see what he has to say!"

I swiftly opened the envelope and pulled out the thick scented paper. "It is an invitation to ride with him in Hyde Park this afternoon."

"Ride with Lord Blakeley!" Mother cried, grabbing her heart with one hand while fanning her face with the other. "Oh, Rose, you must do it. Just think how jealous Mrs. Jepson will be! She has always felt her daughters could land a titled gentleman, but so far, I have seen no progress." She stood up and began pacing the room in her excitement but then suddenly stopped. "Oh, Rose, please tell me that you won't refuse him! It is such an opportunity."

"I won't refuse him, Mama," I said, happy that my mother and I finally agreed on something.

Lord Blakeley arrived in a stylish barouche drawn by two of the most beautiful white mares I had ever seen. The traces on their harnesses were made of supple black leather, with gold scroll detail along the length of them. The blinders were also black, with a gold coat of arms—I assumed the Blakeley coat of arms—delicately etched into the leather.

"Oh, Lord Blakeley, what a beautiful set of horses!" I couldn't help but exclaim.

"I am glad you approve," he said with a smile as he took my hand and placed it around his arm. "I do like to surround myself with beautiful things." His flattery was the same here as it had been at the ballroom, but it felt more personal on the street, without all of the pomp and finery of a ball.

"It is late in the year for the barouche," he admitted, "but it is one of my favorite carriages, and I was hoping to make a good impression on you. You have left me in complete suspense as to how long I am to remain in your good graces, and I definitely would like our acquaintance to continue after today."

"Well, your mares have left me speechless," I said. "I would continue our acquaintance if only for the chance to see them again."

"I look forward to the day that I provide more of a draw for you than my beasts do, but for now, that will have to suffice," Lord Blakeley said with a smile.

Lord Blakeley's coachman helped Johanna and me into the coach. Johanna sat facing the rear, and I sat facing the front. Lord Blakeley took the seat near me. It had been a long time since I had ridden in Hyde Park, and I was looking forward to it.

The park was not as beautiful this time of year as it was during the spring or early fall, when the leaves were colorful and abundant, but it still held its own sense of beauty. Although the leaves had fallen, the grass still held some green, and swans still swam in the Serpentine.

"Let's head east along the banks of the Serpentine," Lord Blakeley told his driver. "I need to find as much beauty as possible for you to enjoy, Miss Davenport," he added in an undertone just to me, "for you have provided so much beauty to my afternoon."

I bit my lip in order to hold in my laughter. Could Lord Blakeley turn any subject into flattery? "Do you drive?" I asked. "Such fine horses should be a pleasure to handle."

"Drive?" Lord Blakeley asked, perhaps taken aback by my question. "I do enjoy a drive here and there, but for the most part, I prefer that my driver do the work. On an afternoon like this, it allows me the opportunity to give my full attention to you."

My laugh escaped. Apparently he could.

"Do I amuse you, Miss Davenport?" Lord Blakeley asked. "I hadn't tried to."

"I laugh because only you can turn a conversation about driving into a compliment," I said.

"Well," he said. "Now who is flattering whom?"

"I didn't mean it as a compliment."

"Ah, but I took it as one. But I won't if you spare me a real one."

"You would like me to compliment you?" I asked.

"I would, very much."

I squinted my eyes, looked him up and down, head to toe, and cocked my head to one side. He sat straighter in his seat, with an expectant look on his face. The movement caused his knee to graze mine slightly.

"You, my lord . . ." I began and then stopped to look him up and down again. I took that opportunity to slide softly away from him. Our knees no longer touched.

"Yes?" He grabbed the edge of the carriage, impatient for my answer.

"You have the most beautiful pair of white mares I have ever seen."

"What?" he said incredulously. "That is a compliment to my horses."

"Ah, but a compliment to one's horses is a true compliment to the owner," I said.

"My horses are still my biggest draw? Not my devilish good looks?" I shook my head no. "My impeccable taste in clothes?" Another shake. "What about my title? Surely being a marquis is nothing to sneeze at." I gave him another shake. "My smile. You can give me credit for having a dashingly good smile."

That one gave me pause, and he noticed. A grin lit his face. The dimple on the right side of his cheek made an appearance. He did have a great smile. Perhaps I should give him that. "I'll tell you just how deserving of praise your smile is if you tell me why you were hiding behind that tree at the Wilmington's ball."

His dimple disappeared at that. "That conversation will not put me in a favorable light, I'm afraid," he said, which, of course, made me want to know even more.

"Should I spend the whole of the outing praising your horses, then?" I said. "Or perhaps their groomer? He has done a fine job maintaining their coats."

Lord Blakeley groaned. "My vanity won't allow that." He pursed his lips and lowered his eyebrows. "I was fixing my cravat."

"You hid behind that tree because . . ."

"My cravat had come slightly loose, yes." I hadn't noticed until now, but his cravat was impressively tied today. His valet must have taken extensive lessons to perform that particular knot.

"My compliments to your valet; he's done a masterful job today."

Lord Blakeley's hand went to his neck, his hand lightly resting on his servant's handiwork. "That wasn't the deal! I didn't just humiliate myself in order to receive a compliment for my valet."

"Your cravat is flawless, Lord Blakeley, and so is your smile." As far as compliments went, it wasn't my best, but Lord Blakeley brightened, producing not only his delightful dimple but also some deep crinkles on the edges of his eyes. Apparently praising his cravat and his looks in one breath had been the right move.

His happiness seemed to warrant another compliment, and I was about to give him one when, out of the corner of my eye, I saw a familiar shape shifting through the crowds of people. His walk seemed a little off, but overall, his body proportions and the silhouette of his face were as familiar as my own. It was William, here at Hyde Park, and he was not alone. Lord Blakeley was talking again, so I laughed without turning to look at him. I assumed he had meant to be entertaining. In truth, I hadn't heard a word he'd said.

William had a dark-haired woman on his arm, and from the looks of it, they were very close. I ignored Lord Blakeley completely as I investigated further. William's hat was pulled down low in an attempt to hide his face from anyone crossing their path, the exact opposite of what most people of the *ton* were doing. I inspected the dark-haired woman; her dress was not at all fashionable and, although it fit shockingly well, was made of rougher fabric than a lady would wear.

They had no carriage but, rather, were walking on the side of the road that was less visited by the ladies and gentlemen of the *ton*. They crossed a bridge, and after looking left and right to make sure nobody was coming, William lifted the woman onto one of the raised stone walls of the bridge. I couldn't hear the peals of her laughter, but I could feel them in the way her body shook as she walked daintily on top of the three-foot wall. William held her hand so she could keep her balance, and her other arm floated in the air as if she were a tightrope walker. When they reached the end of the bridge, he turned to help her down. The woman's skirts blocked my view of his face as she slowly descended toward him. As soon as her feet touched the ground, he scooped her up by the waist and spun her around until I could see only his back. When he set her feet back on the ground, he bent in an unmistakable way. William was kissing the low woman, in Hyde Park, no less!

I could hear Lord Blakeley's voice, but it was only sound, not words. I shook my head in an effort to bring myself back to the carriage, but my eyes wouldn't look anywhere but at the romantic pair at the end of the bridge. Who was this woman William was with, and why did he need to be dressed in what seemed to be a disguise? How could William do this to his family? Had he been secretly courting a woman? I couldn't help but feel that this would explain his indifference to me. But then I immediately felt guilty for thinking of myself first. What of Lady Chatsworth? With one son already in a disaster of a marriage, how could William do this to his family?

My first inclination was to turn away and pretend I hadn't seen anything, but my anger began to build, and I clenched my fists and bit my lower lip. I wanted to confront him. We were nearly adjacent to the bridge they had crossed, and I knew if I didn't think of something right away, I would lose any opportunity I had to catch William with the woman.

"Lord Blakeley, I am so sorry. I sometimes feel ill in carriages." That was true enough. "Would you mind terribly if I took Johanna with me and walked for just a moment to settle my nerves?"

Lord Blakeley looked surprised but quickly instructed his man to pull the barouche over to the side of the road. I had seen the path William and his *lady*—I shuddered at the word—had taken through the park, and I knew I would be able to overtake them.

The footman helped me down, and I quickly made my way to the path, trusting Johanna to follow as quickly as she could. Claiming to be indisposed had its advantages. I assumed Lord Blakeley would not ask me about anything as indelicate as to why I had hurried off.

Tall trees absent of most of their leaves adorned each side of the pathway I marched down. Before long, I had nearly overtaken them. There were a few other couples and gentlemen walking the path, and as much as I wanted to confront William, I didn't want to cause a scene or a scandal for him or his family. When I was only a few feet behind them, I followed them for a while, waiting for a lull in the crowd to actually call out to them. The woman walked with such a bounce in her step, she reminded me of a young girl. The thought was dismissed quickly enough with one look at her figure.

William's walk seemed different. As I continued to watch them, I became more and more certain that I had made a mistake.

I laughed to myself, and the tightness in my arm muscles released. This wasn't William. It couldn't be. I felt mortified that I could have even thought such a thing. Suddenly, there were no other couples around us. I convinced myself to turn around, but just at that moment, the man turned his head and in profile, even with his hat pulled low and his collar high, he certainly looked like William.

I stood there, half turned back toward Lord Blakeley's barouche, but I never completed the turn. I had to know.

"Lord Telford," I hissed low enough that no one else would hear. He immediately stopped. He didn't turn to see who had spoken his name. He seemed to take a deep breath and then pushed his hat lower down onto his head. He protectively steered the woman he was with off to another path in a rush. She turned to him in confusion, but he didn't stop to explain anything to her. They turned a corner out of sight, and my doubt melted away with my hope.

I stopped walking, I stopped breathing, and the only thing I could think was that it was him. It was William, and he was hiding something that was going to tear his family apart.

"Miss Davenport!" Johanna called breathlessly behind me. I turned to look at her, but my eyes wouldn't focus. I could, however, see that she was coming closer to me at an astonishing pace. I shook my head and blinked. "Miss Davenport, you were off so quickly I couldn't keep up. Are you very ill?" I could see her more clearly now, and she looked concerned. "Has your stomach settled?"

"My stomach?" I blinked again. "Ah, yes, my stomach is fine. We should probably return to the barouche." We walked a few steps and ran into Lord Blakeley. He must have also followed us on the path. He took my arm silently, and I was glad to have the support. We walked the path back to the carriage, and no one said a word or asked how I was feeling. It was probably clear enough on my face. After helping me back into the carriage, Lord Blakeley took the seat opposite me instead of near me, as he had on our way through Hyde Park. He must have been worried that I could be ill and believed that seat would be safer.

"Take us back to the Davenport residence," Lord Blakeley instructed the driver without looking at him. I was grateful he didn't want to ride any longer. It must have been only six o'clock, and most of the *ton* would be riding for at least another hour.

It wasn't until I was let down from the carriage after a silent ride home and Lord Blakeley had said his goodbyes that I realized how discourteous I had been for the last quarter of an hour.

"Lord Blakeley," I called back to him as he was about to ascend his carriage. He stopped and turned to look at me. "Thank you so much for the ride. I am sorry to have become so indisposed." He gave me a slight nod, but his smile still seemed far away. "Will you be attending the Langdale ball the day after next?" I asked.

"I was planning on it. Will you be there?"

"I will," I answered, hoping he could see my intention.

"If it would still be agreeable, perhaps you could save the supper dance for me," he said.

"It would be very agreeable," I said, swallowing the feelings of regret and shock that had overtaken me for the last half hour and smiling at him. He seemed to relax. "And thank you for your company today; it is always a pleasure."

"As is yours, Miss Davenport, but next time I wish for your company, which I am confident will be soon after the Langdale ball, I will come and call at your home. I fear our ride in the park has left you open to . . . an affliction, and I would rather not subject you to such suffering again." He gave a short bow, then hopped into his barouche and left with a jovial wave of his walking stick.

CHAPTER 8

"WE ARE FORTUNATE ELIZABETH'S CONNECTIONS were able to secure us an invitation to the Langdale ball," my mother reminded me for the third time as she, my father, and I waited in our carriage to be admitted. "The Langdales are very particular about whom they invite since their ballroom is hardly big enough to allow anyone but top families access," Mother said with a sniff. She was proud of how well her daughters had married, and I knew she had high hopes for me. However, gratitude for attending the ball was the furthest thing from my mind. I still could not get the image of William and the mysterious woman out of my mind.

"I am sure Rose will not forget to thank the hostess for being so magnanimous as to invite her," my father said when I failed to answer. I would have to remember to do that. "Thank the hostess," I whispered to myself.

I had come up with a thousand excuses as to what else the situation could have been. Perhaps it was an act of charity for a young widow. He was the kind of man who could be helpful and kind in a situation and not realize or care what it looked like to an observer. Or perhaps it had been a chance encounter with an old friend or relative. But neither of these speculations carried any weight. They had embraced in a way no self-respecting widow or relative would.

And no matter what excuse I made in my heart, I knew William would never have cause to run away so quickly if he had not been doing something clandestine.

My parents and I climbed the stairs, and I absentmindedly lifted my pale white skirt. There would be no standing out today, and I was glad of it. I wasn't sure I would be capable of regular conversation this evening. Other than Lord Blakeley, whom I was determined to keep up appearances with, any man I danced with tonight could already be counted as a loss.

I bowed to Lady Langdale as my name was announced, properly thanked her, and then moved into the ballroom. The smaller size of the ballroom was compensated by the profuse flowers the Langdales had brought in.

"Is Lord Blakeley here?" my mother asked.

"I was just wondering the same thing," I answered truthfully. I needed to try my best to be charming to him, at least, to make up for our disastrous carriage ride. "I don't see him."

Our gazes wandered the ballroom until my mother started in recognition and pointed to the other side of the ballroom with her fan. "Oh, but there is Lord Telford, so you shall have at least one dance."

I followed my mother's gaze, and sure enough, there he was. William, or rather Lord Telford, smiled at another lord as if he had every right to be here, enjoying an evening of pleasantries while being completely dishonest with his family. His head turned, and I knew the exact moment he caught my eye. His smile faded, and he stopped speaking for a moment. With a shake of his head, he turned back to his companions and, smile returning, finished his conversation.

I continued to watch him, and to my horror, William made his way to us. I absentmindedly ran my hands down the side of my dress to flatten any creases from the carriage ride.

"Sir John! Lady Davenport, it is a pleasure to see you," William said when he reached our corner of the ballroom. I bowed ever so slightly, though perhaps I shouldn't have. It was not as if he had addressed me.

"Lord Telford, good to see you," my father answered. "How is your mother faring?"

"She is in excellent health and hoping to make the drive to London soon," he said. I searched his eyes, trying to find the guilt that must be hiding behind them, but I couldn't see it. He was better at deception than I would have ever thought possible.

How could he talk so casually and happily about his mother's health while harboring a secret that could ultimately destroy it?

"I hope you never give her cause to lose her health, Lord Telford," I said.

He raised an eyebrow at me, his first acknowledgment that I was there. "I have taken great pains to ensure that will never happen, Miss Davenport, I assure you."

"But it shouldn't require *great pains* to please a mother, should it? Not unless you have done something that would be displeasing, anyway."

"Rose!" my mother cried. "Lord Telford hasn't done a displeasing thing in his life! How could you say such a thing?"

"No," Lord Telford replied. "She's right. I am guilty of making errors of judgment and of the heart, just like many other men. If I was a more filial son, I am sure I would have an easier time fulfilling my mother's request."

"Ah, the search for a bride," my father said. "How is that going?"

"I'm just starting. Until Mother arrives, I probably won't make much progress. It's for her sake I am marrying, after all."

"Well, if you aren't hard at work tonight securing some fortunate lady's hand," my mother said, "you must dance with Rose. Her most likely partner is not here, and I would hate to see her a wallflower. She didn't take the care she normally does for an elegant evening like this, and I am rather afraid it shows."

"She looks as beautiful as ever," Lord Telford assured my mother. He didn't look at me as he said it. He had only barely glanced at me at all, so I took no stock in his compliment.

"In other words, Mama, there is no need for Lord Telford to waste a dance on me. An *eligible bachelor* like himself should not be forced into dancing with women who distress him," I said, hoping my words would prick his conscience. "Besides, I am happy to wait for someone else to ask me. No need to foist Lord Telford on me."

"Rose is correct," my father said. "She is perfectly capable of securing her own dances."

"Truly, I am, Mama," I said, and then without a dismissal or even a parting word, I walked away. It was quite possibly the rudest thing I had ever done, but I didn't regret it. Being near William was doing nothing to improve my mood.

I stopped near the refreshment room and looked over the ballroom once again. Elizabeth would be here tonight, as well as Dorothea, but neither of them had arrived yet. I just needed to bide my time until they came, and then I would have someone to talk to or, at the very least, someone to stand near.

"Miss Davenport!" a sickening voice behind me said. I took a deep breath to steel myself, then opened my jaw and slid it to one side, because mother always told me not to grind my teeth. "You look quite fetching this evening." I turned around just in time to receive his compliment directly to my face.

"Thank you, Lord Humphreys," I replied, trying to discreetly wipe my cheek. "You are too kind."

"I am so happy to catch you early in the evening. I hope your supper dance has not yet been spoken for."

I sighed, hoping my sigh sounded like disappointment and not the relief it was. "I am sorry, Lord Humphreys, it has been spoken for," I said, grateful that Lord Blakeley had asked me for it.

"Spoken for so early . . ." Lord Humphreys said with one eye drooped in skepticism, or did it always droop? I couldn't remember. "I've had my eye on you ever since you entered, and you've hardly spoken to anyone."

I slid my jaw to the left this time. It wasn't polite to question a lady. Fortunately, I was telling the truth and could set him straight.

"She spoke to me," William said, coming up from behind me. My teeth clinked as my jaw snapped shut and I gritted my teeth. "Perhaps I am the one who has claim on that dance."

"Lord Telford," I said, giving him my second cursory bow of the evening. He returned my bow with a nod and a smile that belied our unfortunate interaction at his home just weeks ago. I wanted nothing more than to ignore him this evening. I would have thought he would feel the same.

"Is that true, Miss Davenport? Is he the one who has been promised the supper dance?" Lord Humphreys asked.

"No," I said. "He only said *perhaps*. Lord Telford was rather pressed to ask me to dance, but I am afraid he never actually did." William seemed taken aback at my reply. He thought he was doing me a favor. I felt my lips curl in satisfaction. I was perfectly capable of taking care of myself. I didn't need his charity. "I'm afraid I have promised the supper dance to someone else."

"Well, then, the first dance?" Lord Humphreys said. "Has that been spoken for?"

"No, I am happy to save that one for you," I said to Lord Humphreys. He smiled a gap-toothed grin at Lord Telford, as if he had just won a prize. With a sloppy kiss on my glove, he left to find some other unfortunate young lady to ask for the supper dance.

"You didn't have to tell him you had promised that dance to someone else. I would have been happy to dance with you," William said as soon as Lord Humphreys walked away.

"You've never bothered to dance with me before. And besides, I couldn't very well tell him that as I *have* promised the supper dance already."

William narrowed one eye at me in disbelief, and I nearly lost control of my tenuous composure. William was judging *me* for being deceptive.

"*Miss Davenport*, I have watched you for two years dance with men from all stations, and I have yet to see you give preference to any of them. I highly doubt you would have promised the supper dance before the ball." He paused, and I balled my fists, determined to not be goaded by him. "If you didn't want to dance with me, you could have just mentioned it. You didn't have to mislead poor Lord Humphreys."

"You are correct in assuming I have no desire to dance with you," I replied. "A man who harbors secrets that will sorely disappoint his family and hurt his mother tremendously is not an attractive one to me. Besides, I know you are not free, and now that I know, I cannot unknow it."

"What in the world are you alluding to? What secret?" He sounded quite convincing until he added, "Who have you been talking to?"

I had no desire to listen to William try to play innocent. I spotted Lord Blakeley across the room. He was glaring at Lord Telford. "There is Lord Blakeley now. You needn't concern yourself any longer about my lack of dance partner." I smiled at Lord Blakeley, and he started coming our direction.

"Lord Blakeley?" William said incredulously. He must have been surprised that someone of Lord Blakeley's caliber would be interested in pursuing me. "After two years of searching, Lord Blakeley is the one who finally catches your eye?" William looked completely taken aback.

"Why should that surprise you?" I asked.

"Lord Blakeley?" he said, shaking his head, putting his index finger to his lower lip and sliding it back and forth in thought.

"Yes, Lord Blakeley," I said. What could William possibly have against Lord Blakeley?

"But the man has two wooden teeth!"

"He does not!" I hissed at him.

"He does. Ask him. He lost them in a riding accident!"

"I could never ask him that! Besides, a few wooden teeth wouldn't bother me," I said with my shoulders thrown back and my spine stiff.

But frustratingly, I found it did.

"But it does, doesn't it, Rose?" William said. His left eyebrow was cocked over his all-knowing eye.

"*Do not* use my Christian name here, Lord Telford, or ever again. We are no longer children, and we have no relation. It's completely inappropriate." William stepped away from me as if I had slapped him. It was almost as satisfying as if I had.

Lord Blakeley was nearly to us, and I smiled my most dazzling smile at him. I was certain I had never smiled at William that way. It had the intended effect. William scowled, and Lord Blakeley's mouth spread wide in a large, toothy grin. I couldn't help but look closely at his teeth. The two in front did seem a little darker than the others.

My smile must have faltered as I inspected him, for William chuckled lightly as he bowed to Lord Blakeley. "Lord Blakeley," William said.

"Lord Telford," Lord Blakeley replied with a cursory nod before addressing me. "Miss Davenport, is everything all right? You seemed distressed."

"I'm fine," I said. "Lord Telford was just leaving." Both Lord Blakeley and I turned expectantly to William, who took the hint with a shrug of his shoulders and turned to leave.

"Is he the man you met in Hyde Park?" Lord Blakeley asked, and I saw William's step falter. He turned to look at us with his eyes narrowed. He may not have known that it was me who had called out to him in Hyde Park, but now he would.

I didn't know how to respond. I hadn't been aware that Lord Blakeley had even known I had seen someone at the park that day. "When I saw you from across the room, you had the same discouraged look about you as you did that afternoon," Lord Blakeley said.

William stopped glaring at us and walked farther away, out of earshot.

"I didn't actually meet anyone in Hyde Park," I answered truthfully, but at Lord Blakeley's raised eyebrow, I expounded. "But I did see someone, and you are correct in assuming the encounter left me unnerved."

"But you would rather not talk about it," he supplied, and I was grateful for it.

"I would rather not talk about it," I said. "I would like to thank you, though, for inadvertently saving me from Lord Humphreys a second time."

"Did I?"

"Oh yes," I said. "If you hadn't invited me for the supper dance, I would be stuck not only dancing with him but accompanying him to supper as well."

"Well, if that is the case, the pleasure is all mine," Lord Blakeley said. "It is only a pity I will have to wait so long to claim that dance. I hope one day to not have to settle for just one dance per ball with you, Miss Davenport."

I kept my smile stretched across my face, so I hoped Lord Blakeley didn't notice any change in my countenance. At his words, I suddenly felt as if I had been too long in a carriage. There was a good chance I was going to be running from Lord Blakeley just like I had last year. His attention had felt needed after my confidence-killing encounter with William outside his bedchamber. But if Lord Blakeley were to ask for a second dance tonight, I knew I would have to say no. And it wasn't just because of his wooden teeth.

"But that day is not today, is it?" Lord Blakeley stated.

"No, Lord Blakeley, not today."

He changed the subject, and we discussed the latest opera until it was time for Lord Humphreys to claim me for the first dance.

I gritted my teeth as he and I found a place on the ballroom floor. He must have taken great pains with his hair this evening, as I could smell bear fat each time we reached a point in the dance when our hands touched. The few strands of hair remaining on the top of his head were pressed flat and were slicked back against his unfortunate crown. Even still, I found myself relaxing as we danced. I was happy not to have to come up with anything witty to say. I wasn't eager to be interesting to Lord Humphreys, and even if I was, I was quite certain cleverness was not the best way to catch his eye.

The evening seemed to drag, and even the supper dance with Lord Blakeley didn't restore my spirits. Supper was a chore as I tried to keep up with conversations. I was more than ready to leave by the time the meal was over, but I knew my mother was correct and this was an exclusive ball. No matter how terrible I felt, we needed to put our best foot forward. Leaving early wasn't an option.

I sat beside Elizabeth while the dancing continued after supper. I was happy to have a few free dances in a row so I could just sit and speak with my sister. My mood had not escaped her.

"Are you feeling unwell?" Elizabeth asked.

"Is it that noticeable?" I asked in return, slowly closing my eyes. "I know how important this ball is for Mama."

"I imagine not many people would realize it, but I know you well enough to see it. It's as if the regular you has been dulled. You usually shine in a crowd, like a diamond among rough stones. Tonight I've had a hard time finding you."

I sighed and hoped Elizabeth was the only one astute enough to realize my true feelings about this ball. I gave her a large smile. "How's this?" I asked.

"It would be more believable if you relaxed your hands."

I looked down to see that both of my hands were balled into fists. I stretched out my fingers, willing them to be loose and relaxed.

"Just a few more hours," Elizabeth promised in a whisper. "Then you will be able to go home."

Just a few more hours. We didn't have any large occasions planned for the next few days. Perhaps with some rest, I would be able to enjoy the next ball.

"Lord Telford!" Elizabeth beckoned to William behind me. I turned to see that he was headed our way with a smile plastered on his face. I looked at his hands. Unlike mine, they were relaxed. Perhaps he was actually enjoying the ball. Plenty of women had been making eyes at him all evening. For a man who needed to be engaged soon, he seemed to pay them no mind. It must have been difficult to feign interest while his heart was attached elsewhere. "Lord Telford will cheer you up. You were always such good friends."

My involuntary smile became even more forced.

"Lady Hawthorne, Miss Davenport," William said, addressing us.

"It's good to see you, Lord Telford. How are your parents?" Elizabeth asked.

"They are doing well," William answered with that same rehearsed smile.

"Rose is having a rather dull time this evening," Elizabeth whispered, and I grabbed her wrist, hoping to stop her from what I felt was coming. "Why don't you invite her for a dance? It will do her some good to spend time with a friend."

William raised his eyebrow at me. I imagined his thoughts to be the same as my own. *Why does everyone assume we are friends?*

"Oh, Elizabeth, Mama already tried to talk William into dancing with me, and it is of no use. He hasn't danced with me over the course of two seasons, and there is no reason to start now."

"Perhaps there is a reason now." Elizabeth lowered her voice so only he and I could hear. "Mama told me about Lord Telford's agreement with his mother. I see no reason why he should spend so much time looking for a wife when you two already get along famously."

William turned white, and his casual smile disappeared. Elizabeth couldn't know that he had already informed me of how unsuitable that situation would be.

"Elizabeth," I hissed. "That is much more inappropriate than you could ever imagine. Get the idea of Wil—Lord Telford—and I connected in *any* way out of your mind. It is impossible."

Elizabeth just laughed. "All right, all right. No need to have a fit over it," she said. "It seemed like a good solution to me, but if you aren't interested, you aren't interested."

"I am not interested," I reiterated.

"Not at all?" William asked quietly. I blushed slightly at the thought of my early-morning visit to his room. What must he have thought of me?

"Not at all," I said, making my voice even and calm.

He nodded. "In that case, I will ask you to dance. Would you do me the honor of dancing with me for the next set?" William asked.

My hands relaxed, and for a moment, the music in the room seemed to soften, as if somehow, simultaneously, all the musicians had lost a portion of their strength and couldn't produce the volume they had just seconds before. I had spent my whole first season hoping for that exact question only to get it now that I knew he was unattainable. I wasn't interested in him, and because of that, he finally felt comfortable enough to ask me. It made sense. As an attached man, he should want only to dance with uninterested women, which would be fine if I could actually *feel* uninterested. My mind rehearsed the scene in the park, continuously reminding me that I should feel nothing toward him. My heart, however, kept noticing things like his familiar gray eyes and the fine cut of his jacket moving over arms that I should never have explored. I bit my lip, and Elizabeth gave me a nudge.

"I will," I answered, wishing my voice could be stronger.

The cotillion in progress was far from over, which meant I should probably say something to William. He was just standing there. What does one speak about with a person she possibly used to care for but who now was deceiving all of his friends and family and who was forever out of her grasp? I sat there awkwardly trying to think of a topic that could be safe to bring up.

"Are you absolutely certain they are wooden?" I asked after the silence became unbearable.

"Positive," he answered, and I sighed, which seemed to make him happy.

Elizabeth quirked her eyebrows at me, and I just shook my head. I wasn't going to tell her William's gossip.

"We have some time before the next dance. Should we take some refreshment?" William asked, and since anything would be better than just standing or sitting here with nothing to say, I agreed. Elizabeth declined with a small shake of her head. William took my hand to raise me out of my chair.

"Perhaps they have petit fours . . ." William whispered to me when I was standing, and I almost laughed. He lifted his arm for me to take it, and habitually, I reached up to grab it, but then halfway there, I remembered the encounter in the park and dropped my hands to my side. It took William a moment to realize I was rejecting his arm before he hastily set it down.

When we arrived in the refreshment room, I realized I would not be capable of eating, so I asked only for a punch. I could feel William standing behind me, and I tried to ignore the draw I had always felt for him. Twice, I caught myself leaning back to be closer to him, but I stopped myself before I could do anything quite that publicly embarrassing. The final strains of the cotillion played. The time for stalling was gone. William and I were finally going to have a dance.

The music stopped, and this time, when William reached for my arm, he didn't wait for me to take it. Instead, he grasped my hand and wrapped it around his forearm as he escorted me to the ballroom and onto the floor. I tried not to notice the firmness of his grip and how he managed to trap my hand with his arm in a motion that was both proprietary and soothing at the same time. It was us crossing the stream all over again, and even though our clothes were dry, I felt that we were much more uncomfortable tonight than we had been after only knowing each other for a few awkward days. I thought about pulling away but decided instead to relax and not cause a scene.

We finally reached our destination, a small group on the outside edge of the ballroom. I recognized no one. His grip on me loosened, and I quickly dropped my arm. As my hand fell, my fingers lightly grazed the palm of his hand in an accidental touch. He flinched at the contact.

"Did I overhear Lord Blakeley say you met a man in Hyde Park?" he asked just as the music was about to start. He said it innocently, as if asking only out of curiosity.

"You might have, if you were listening to our private conversation," I said, curious as to why he would have even brought the subject up. It was hardly dance conversation.

"I couldn't help but overhear it," William said. "You really should be more careful about what you say in company."

Oh, I thought, *he wants to make sure I won't tell anyone.* "First of all, I wasn't the one who said anything, and secondly, if you want me to keep quiet about what I saw in Hyde Park, you need only ask," I said to him, hoping to end this conversation as quickly as possible.

"Of course you should keep quiet about it. Can you imagine the repercussions if such news got out?" His face was suddenly lines. Lines between his eyes and even deeper lines on either side of his mouth.

"I see that you are imagining them," I said.

"How could I not?" he asked, looking askance at me, and a deep growl started to form somewhere in my chest. I wasn't going to tell anyone what I had seen. I pushed the snarl back down—growling would be highly inappropriate for a lady at a ball—but he should have trusted me not to expose his secret.

"It seems to me," I said, proud of my steady voice, "that if you were so worried about the consequences of personal decisions, you should have made a point to prevent such things from happening." I don't know what else he expected from me.

"I'm sorry," he replied, pulling his head back. "I see no possible way in which I could have controlled your behavior enough to prevent this."

"My behavior?" I asked, but then the dancing started, and I was unable to continue. I stepped away from William, but I was still seething. I managed to complete my steps—twist, turn, and steps by threes—until we ended back at the side and could speak again. "I am innocent in all of this! I didn't plan on that incident in the park," I hissed at him as soon as I had the chance. "And you should know better. The choices you are making are going to make your family miserable."

His eyebrows furrowed at my accusation. "How can you say that when every choice I am making now goes against my own wishes in order to make them happy?" he asked.

"But you must see that your deceptiveness can only lead to heartache in the end for everyone you love." William must understand this. There was no way he could keep this secret indefinitely. I expected him to be angry at my words, but instead, he was looking at me as if I had grown a second head. I didn't understand how my words could be surprising. Surely the thought was not new to him.

The time came for us to take up our steps again, but he didn't move. I grabbed his hand, but instead of guiding me back into the dance, he pulled my hand back and away from the dancers. I glanced around the room. No one except the others in our set noticed our misstep. If we hurried, perhaps we wouldn't cause much of a scene. I pulled on William's hand once more, but he only held it tighter, unmoving.

"You're right," he said, quietly pulling me off to the side and away from the dancing. He led me through a few other dancers on the outer periphery of the room, and I was glad we had not been in the center of the room. Lord Blakeley was dancing off to one side, glaring at us. I shrugged my shoulders in his direction. Hopefully he understood that I wasn't the one who had instigated this. When we got near the wall, William still pulled me this way and that until he found an unpopulated corner. He led me there and stood scandalously close to me, but at least he did drop my hand.

"Of course you are right. But I don't know how to fix any of this, Rose." He ran his hand through his hair, probably not the greatest idea at a ball, but he didn't seem to care. He looked so desperate I felt an instant need to help him, but I knew it was not my place to comfort him. "I am not Joseph. I cannot disappoint my parents like he did."

"You should have thought of that sooner, Lord Telford," I said, trying to keep the compassion I felt out of my voice.

"What do you mean by that?" he asked, looking genuinely confused. How could he not know the thing to do in his situation was to either confess and explain to his parents that he was attached or call things off with the woman in the park?

"What do I mean?" I asked him. "When your older brother accused you of not being a man, I always thought he was being ridiculous. I thought I knew you better. Are you really so incapable of making up your own mind? There are only two choices for you now. You can give up the woman you love, or you can tell your family about her." For the second time in the evening, William reacted as if I had slapped him. His face dropped, and he took a step away from me. This time, however, I felt no satisfaction. Just a sick twisting in my gut.

"Perhaps I am spineless," he finally answered. "No, I know I am. These past few years have been excruciating for me. But I never thought it mattered to you. And truthfully, even if it does, I am not sure if there is anything I can do about it. My hands are tied, Rose. My situation cannot allow for any attachment between us."

I felt heat rise to my face. Did he think I was speaking to him about this because I wanted him to be free for me to pursue? "Believe me, Wil—Lord Telford—I am completely aware of that. Please don't assume I would care for any sort of attachment with you. I am sorry and embarrassed if anything I said seemed to convey a feeling toward you that isn't—cannot be—there."

"Oh," he replied slowly. "I thought . . . Well, good, then." He cleared his throat. "I am sorry, truly sorry if I alluded to any sort of attachment on your part. Of course it was ridiculous. How could you care for someone as weak-willed as me?"

"Right," I answered just as slowly, not sure how our conversation had reached this point. But I was glad to set things straight, especially since he might have assumed things from my early-morning visit to him at his home.

"You should probably find Lord Blakeley," he said. "I saw him glaring at us a few moments ago. You can just explain to him that I had a momentary fit of madness but that I won't bother you again." He reached for my hand and held it up to his lips. Before kissing it, he ran his thumb slowly over each knuckle. After a brief touch to his mouth, he dropped my hand and walked off stiffly, his shoulders back and his head up as if he were a soldier marching into a battle he knew he wouldn't win. I hoped he wouldn't do anything rash. Perhaps I shouldn't have encouraged him to stand up to his family and let them know about his private life.

William had been right about Lord Blakeley's concern. He found me just a few moments later as I was still puzzling over the conversation I had just had with William.

"Are you all right?" he asked.

"I'm fine," I replied, feeling anything but.

"Let's go find your sister," he said kindly, and I nodded my head.

Elizabeth took one look at my face as we approached and said, "It looks as though the dance with Lord Telford did not, in fact, leave you feeling better."

"I'm not feeling well at all," I told Elizabeth when we reached her. "I probably should never have come tonight."

"Let's go find Mama; she will take you home."

"You and I both know that isn't true. She will be one of the last to leave," I said.

"I am certain when she sees your state, she will see the need to leave early. No one would fault your family for leaving due to illness," Lord Blakeley said.

Elizabeth and I both gave him a look that said otherwise.

"Come home with me, then," Elizabeth said. "I have no one to impress here. Charles would be happy to have you stay tonight, and even if he isn't, a chance to leave any ball early would make him gratified enough to bear it. Mama can send the carriage to pick you up tomorrow."

"Thank you, Elizabeth," I said.

CHAPTER 9

I WAS SETTLED INTO ELIZABETH'S guest room, trying to keep from seeing William and that woman in the park every time I closed my eyes, when a soft knock came on the door. I knew it must be Elizabeth, and I was grateful that she would come check on me.

"Come in!" I called out to her, not wanting to leave the warmth of my bed.

Elizabeth, also in her nightdress, snuck quietly into my room.

"Climb on up," I invited, and she wasted no time jumping into the bed, scooting me over to enjoy the warmest part of the bed.

"I'm glad you are here," Elizabeth said. "I miss spending evenings together like we used to."

"Yes, well, we could still be doing this if horrible Charles hadn't snatched you up."

"Yes," Elizabeth agreed. "Horrible Charles." Her face softened as she mentioned his name, and she said, "Perhaps I should just get back to him." She started to leave, and I pulled her back down.

"Oh, no you don't! He can suffer an evening alone for a change. He gets you all the time."

"I was only jesting. I am sure he is snoring like a lion already. I really do want to talk to you. Are you quite ill?"

"Not ill," I replied, "but I am sick at heart, I suppose."

"Has some man treated you badly?" she asked. "Charles would be happy to avenge you in any way. He cleans his pistols regularly, hoping for a chance to use them on some poor fool."

"No," I replied, though not completely assured her story about Charles was in jest. "I have not been ill used. I'm afraid I am only now coming to understand my heart, and unfortunately, it is breaking."

"Am I safe to assume this isn't about Lord Blakeley?"

"You are."

"The only person I have ever seen you search for in a crowded ballroom is Lord Telford. Was I wrong to make him dance with you tonight?"

"Oh, Elizabeth, you couldn't have known, but truly, it was the most wretched dance of my life," I said, pulling my face lower under the covers.

"Do you dislike Lord Telford so much? I thought you had become friends at Feldstone."

"I wish I disliked him! It would make all of this so much easier."

"He seemed happy enough to oblige you with a dance." Elizabeth propped herself up on her elbow.

"His heart is not free," I said with a shake of my head. "I saw him with a woman, one obviously inferior to him, at Hyde Park. She was absolutely stunning, even in her shoddy clothes."

"You must be mistaken. There is no way Lord Telford would pursue a woman that far beneath him. He saw what happened to his brother."

"But if he truly loved her? What other choice would he have?"

"Lord Telford wouldn't. I don't know him well, but everything I know of the man tells me this would be completely out of character for him. I mean, even Charles compliments him." She raised her eyebrows. "Charles!" She placed a strong emphasis on her husband's name. "He never compliments anyone."

"How does Charles even know Lord Telford?" I couldn't help but ask. "I am surprised Charles would have an opinion of him at all."

"The Chatsworth townhome is just down the street," Elizabeth said.

"Oh," I said. "I guess I should have known his family would live in Grosvenor Square."

"At any rate, Charles knows him quite well and has never had a bad word to say about him. Surely you must be wrong."

"I saw it with my own eyes, Elizabeth."

"Perhaps your eyes were mistaken. Are you quite certain it was him?"

"He was dressed differently than usual—I suppose to help him remain incognito. At first, I also doubted it could be him," I said. "But when I called out his name, he jumped and then ran off. There would be no reason for anyone else to do that."

"I still believe you're wrong," Elizabeth continued. "The way he looks at you reminds me of Charles when we were courting. I could never fully believe that a man like him could care for me, but look at us now—married, with a two-year-old son."

"William is no Charles, and I am definitely no Elizabeth. I don't expect to find a match quite as happy as yours, but still, I would rather not have to watch as a man I have found myself attracted to ruins his life for another woman. Even if she is as beautiful as a spring morning . . . Actually, especially if she is as beautiful as a spring morning. Does that make me odious?"

Elizabeth laughed, and I found comfort in the familiar reverberation of her throat. "That makes you human," she said. "You will find someone, Rose. I cannot imagine any woman being more beautiful than you, and your beauty is not even your greatest feature."

"You should have seen her."

"It wouldn't have mattered if I had. At every ball, you are the most stunning woman in the room, and I don't only say that because it's true. I also say it because I love you. When you love someone, they become infinitely more handsome." Elizabeth lay back down on the bed and began to gently rub my scalp. I couldn't help but close my eyes tightly, hoping to keep the tears behind my eyelids.

The feel of her hands on my head was both delicious and excruciating. I tried to bask in the feeling of being truly loved by someone, but at the same time, Elizabeth's habit of head rubbing was what started all of this in the first place.

"Someday, you will meet a man who will think you're beautiful no matter what, because that is what love does to people." Her fingers continued in the patterns I knew so well, and slowly, I began to relax. I deepened my breathing so she would assume I was asleep and then steeled myself for what I knew was coming. I felt the bed shift as she quietly bent over my head and placed a soft kiss at my temple. "Good night, Rose," she whispered as she crawled out of the bed.

I waited until the door closed behind her to let my tears fall.

Breakfast at Elizabeth and Charles's home was always a treat. Charles couldn't have cared less about societal rules, and he had completely converted Elizabeth to his depraved ways. At home, Mama required that only the well-behaved could sit together at the table. As a younger child, I'd always taken breakfast in the nursery.

Charles came bounding into the room with little James clinging to his neck from behind. He jumped from side to side, ensuring that James had to use all his might to keep a hold on him. I smiled at Elizabeth, but she wasn't looking at me. She was watching her little family with a look of pure contentment.

"Good morning, wife!" Charles exclaimed as he reached her, bending to give her a quick kiss on the cheek. He then bent over in an awkward position so his son could reach her cheek as well.

"Good morning, Mama!" James's sweet two-year-old voice chirped in the exact tone as his father. I knew this was a morning ritual, and it gave me a quiet longing to create memories of my own with a family of my own. I had often thought about leaving home before but never because I desired to create something. It was more of a desire to escape the confines of my own upbringing.

Perhaps my late-night talk with Elizabeth had affected me more than I'd realized.

Mrs. Dirksen, the housekeeper, knocked quietly and then entered the room with a letter. She handed it to Charles. "It is for Lady Hawthorne," she announced.

"Let her have it, then. Can't you see I'm occupied?" Charles said, jerking his head in the direction of his wife. Mrs. Dirksen gave a sniff. She didn't seem to approve of Charles's behavior. After waiting a moment to see if Charles would check to see whom the letter was from—he didn't—she delivered it to Elizabeth.

"It's from Mama," we both said simultaneously. Elizabeth ripped open the letter, and I sighed, wondering what Mother could want now. Elizabeth read it first, looked quite pleased, and then handed the note to me.

Elizabeth,

For once, your husband's lack of propriety was of use. I am glad you could take Rose into your home last night. The ball was wonderful, and I know it wouldn't have looked good for your father and me to leave early. Unfortunately, I will need the carriage this morning, as I have heard from Mrs. Jepson that the milliner has had a fine new hat imported from France with a new design no one has heard of here. I really must get there and buy it before anyone else has the chance. (Especially Mrs. Jepson!) Could you either provide Rose with a carriage ride home or come and meet me on Bond Street, where she would be welcome to ride home with me?

Love etc.,
Mother

My disappointment at being considered worth less than a hat, no matter how new and unique, was barely felt before Elizabeth piped up.

"Let's go to Bond Street! It has been ages since we shopped together. If we hurry, perhaps we can beat Mama to that hat."

"I didn't know you were that interested in hats, Elizabeth," I said.

"Oh, I don't care a fig for the hat, but can you imagine the look on Mama's face if we are the ones to purchase it?"

"I like this idea," I said with a smile.

"So do I, Elizabeth," Charles said while feeding the last bite of a crumpet to James, who was still on his shoulder. Charles's morning coat was covered in crumbs. "You don't spend enough of my grandfather's hard-earned money."

"I'm fairly certain your grandfather never worked very hard for his money," Elizabeth answered.

"Elizabeth!" I said, shocked.

"Well, it's true! The Hawthorne money goes back many more generations than that. Charles, it is insulting to imply that your grandfather had to labor for what he had," Elizabeth said.

Charles laughed out loud, causing James to hold on tighter around his neck. "That is true. His hands were as soft as a lady's. Sorry, Grandfather!" Charles looked up to the ceiling as he shouted the words. "I didn't mean to insult your memory in order to convince my wife to buy a hat."

"I should get dressed if we are going to beat Mama," I said, scuttling out of the room with a smile. Sometimes Charles's ridiculousness was too much even for me.

Elizabeth took the challenge to deprive Mama of her hat quite seriously. She dressed quickly and sent her maid to help me much sooner than I had expected her. We were in her carriage and headed to Bond Street in no time.

We arrived at the milliner's shop just as it was opening, but when we walked through the door, we were disappointed to see we were not the first ones there.

"This style is like nothing seen here," the milliner said to her customer, whose back was toward us. They stood near the counter, and the milliner held the incomparable hat up in the air to better show off its features. The customer was much too thin and tall to be Mama, and our mother wouldn't have needed any convincing to buy the hat, although perhaps she should have. The style certainly was like nothing seen in London. The hat was covered in a deep magenta cloth, with multiple feathers parading on top of it. One on each side and, heaven forbid, one right down the middle. Every feather had been dyed a different color. They were full and, quite honestly, ridiculous. Ribbons were bowed all along the brim, and more trailed down the sides.

"I don't know that you should spend the Hawthorne money on that," I said, bending so my mouth was by Elizabeth's ear.

"Shh, don't you remember? The point isn't to like that hat; it's to buy it before Mama does. But it seems as though we might be too late."

We heard the woman say she would take the hat, and then she turned.

"Lady Chatsworth!" I cried out in surprise. I knew she had planned to come to London, but still, it seemed so strange to find her here, looking the picture of health.

"Oh, Rose!" she said. "It is so good to see you!"

"You look so well," I couldn't help but say. Despite my melancholy, I felt some elation at seeing her looking so vibrant.

"Yes, well, I have had some pleasant news, and I suppose it must show on my face," Lady Chatsworth said.

"Pleasant news?" I asked.

"Oh, yes, the best news, really, but I really mustn't say what, I'm afraid. Lord Chatsworth doesn't know yet. Everything is still so new; I just found out last night." The smile on her face fell, and a shadow of worry crossed it.

I fiddled with the buttons on my navy jacket. I knew the news she looked forward to most was an engagement for William. I couldn't make myself ask any further questions, even though I was hoping to be proven wrong. The milliner handed Lady Chatsworth her hat all packed up. Elizabeth must have noticed my complete lack of functionality and decided to engage Lady Chatsworth in a safer subject matter.

"That is quite a hat you have purchased," my sister said to Lady Chatsworth.

"Do you think so? I am worried it might be a bit much."

"It is quite interesting, for certain," Elizabeth said. "As long as you find the right dress to wear it with, it will be quite becoming on you."

"Oh, it isn't for me . . ." she began and then quickly stopped herself. She looked back and forth between Elizabeth and me. "Oh, this just isn't going to do," she said with her face scrunched up. "We can't just keep this a secret forever."

"Has Lord Telford . . . ?" I began in a whisper so quiet I wasn't sure Lady Chatsworth could hear me. I couldn't ask it, I realized. I couldn't ask Lady Chatsworth if the reason she was so vibrant today was because William had taken my advice and told his mother about the woman he was in love with. But it made complete sense. Whom else could she be buying that hat for? Lord Chatsworth would be furious at William's choice for a bride, so of course they wouldn't have told him. I grabbed Elizabeth's arm. I just wanted to leave the shop. I couldn't trust myself to speak with Lady Chatsworth any longer.

"Lady Hawthorne, Miss Davenport," Lady Chatsworth said, stopping us from heading out the door as I had wished. "You and your families must come visit with our family this weekend while Parliament is on break. We will be returning to Feldstone for a few days, perhaps longer. There's someone I would love for you to meet, and I believe your family will be a good buffer between them and Lord Chatsworth."

I pulled on Elizabeth harder. She wanted us to be a buffer for "them"—William and his dark-haired beauty. There was no other answer. Lady Chatsworth wanted us there at the manor so Lord Chatsworth wouldn't run for his gun like he had for Joseph. A new fear entered my heart. Lord Chatsworth wouldn't, would he? What had I pushed William into doing? My memory flashed back to that night as his head lay in my lap, our last night as friends. He had thought his father could forgive Joseph if only he had told them of the marriage before it had occurred. Perhaps that would be enough to save William from total disgrace with his family. At least he wasn't married yet.

"I am sorry to interrupt, Lady Chatsworth," Elizabeth said after looking at my face. "We are to meet our mother soon and must be on our way."

I nodded in agreement, and finally, Elizabeth moved toward the door.

"Oh, yes, you must go meet her," Lady Chatsworth said. "Send her my regards, and I will send an invitation for dinner to your home. The trip from London is not far. I am counting on you to be there!"

We reached the door of the shop, and I wrenched it open. I gulped in the outside air as if I had been suffocating in the milliner's shop.

"I cannot go, Elizabeth," I told her as we walked away. My arm squeezed hers as tightly as a girdle. If I relaxed my grip at all, I was afraid I would fall. "You must see that I cannot go. It is that woman she wants to introduce us to. How will I smile and keep up appearances while Lady Chatsworth uses our family to keep her husband from killing William?"

"Would you rather he actually kill William?" Elizabeth asked.

"No! Of course not! But she must have other friends she can invite over. I have been ill. There is no possible way I can attend, and I will tell Mama."

"I hope that will work for you, Rose," she said. "If not, I will be there. You have two days to prepare. Close off your heart, and think of a man who is better than William. You know he must be out there."

"A man better than William?" I said. "I am not convinced someone like that will be easy to find. I would be happy to find one as good as William, as kind as he was before he became heir." I was going to have to find a man like that, for after knowing William, it would be hard to settle for anything less.

"Let's find something to spend the Hawthorne money on, or Charles will be quite disappointed in me," Elizabeth said.

We visited several other shops, and Elizabeth ordered a new set of gloves and slippers. Nothing caught my eye. When we were finally able to catch up to Mother, she was distraught over having missed her chance to buy that horrendous hat. Neither of us had the heart to tell her who had bought it.

"It must have been Mrs. Jepson. She is bound and determined to stand out so her daughter can snag a title."

"Well, she would stand out in such a hat," Elizabeth said with a snicker.

"We assume . . . based on your description of it," I quickly added with a sideways glance at Elizabeth.

"Mother, why don't you come to my home and have some tea? James would love a visit from his grandmother," Elizabeth said.

Mother glanced longingly down Bond Street at all the shops she hadn't set foot in yet. "I was hoping to get a little more shopping done . . ."

"Well, what if I took Rose home with me, and you stopped by to fetch her when you finish? I think we have both done all the shopping we needed to."

"That would work quite well. In fact, if you could have little James take tea with the two of you beforehand, then I will be able to take mine in peace. I never have understood why you are so adamant about children joining the adults for mealtimes."

"But he would love to see you," Elizabeth said, not bothering to cover her disappointment.

"I will pop into the nursery before I leave. Of course I want to *see* the boy. It is just the noise of children that distresses me." Mother already had her eye on the next shop she wanted to visit, so we bid her farewell, and Elizabeth and I made our way to the carriage. We both sat on the same side of the carriage, and the footman handed us a blanket to share. We settled comfortably into the warmth of our body heat.

"If I ever get to the point where the sound of children is distressing to me, will you please see to it that I am shipped overseas?" Elizabeth whispered to me.

I stared at her in shock. I was usually the one who complained about Mother. I guess when she insulted Elizabeth's flesh and blood, Mama had taken it too far.

"She could be worse, I suppose," I said.

"That's a lovely compliment to give to one's own mother," Elizabeth said, still upset. "But I know you are right. We never really were lacking anything growing up."

"And she gave us each other. For that, I can forgive a multitude of other faults."

"That's true," Elizabeth said. "But she also gave us Dorothea," she said, making a face.

"Elizabeth! Insulting both a mother and a sister in one conversation! Today must be an exemplary day. Perhaps I am a bad influence on you."

"Most likely," she said, snuggling closer to me under the blanket. "But as Charles would say, surrounding yourself with bad influences is a certain way to recognize a good influence when you see it."

"So that is why you enjoy spending time with me," I said with mock disappointment.

"What other reason could there be?"

The carriage rolled on for a few minutes, and I noticed we were nearing Grosvenor Square. As the street opened into the square, I inspected the stately homes. One of these was William's. It was strange to me that my family had never visited his family here in London. I suppose it was because there wasn't hunting to be done anywhere nearby.

"What in heaven's name is going on at the home next to ours?" Elizabeth had been looking at the opposite side of the square. I turned my attention to that home, the last one in a long line of attached residences. I looked across the large oval garden to see a crowd of people gathering. Most of them were the elegant people of Grosvenor Square, but I also noticed a chimney sweep, recognizable from the soot on his hands and face. Next to him stood a brick mason. The bricklayer was frantically setting up scaffolding along the side of the home. Directly above the scaffolding was a chimney.

My heart fell to my feet, and I grabbed the side of the carriage for support. I had heard about situations like this before. I hoped it wasn't what I believed it to be but could think of no other plausible explanation. “Elizabeth, let’s get you home to James. You can send the footman to ask what is going on if you are curious,” I said, trying to keep my voice steady. “It wouldn’t do to be seen gawking at the neighbor’s home.”

“You are probably right,” Elizabeth said. “I will send John to go check on the situation as soon as we arrive home. Perhaps someone is in need of help.”

I nodded as if the situation were a completely normal one. We made our way up the stairs of her stately three-story townhome and went inside. I didn’t remove my coat. “I will go talk to John, Elizabeth. I will be back in a moment to apprise you of what is happening.” Thankfully, Elizabeth just gave me a nod and made her way up the stairs.

CHAPTER 10

"John," I called to the tall, lanky footman as I made my way down the stairs. He turned from his work at the carriage. "Will you accompany me to the home next door? Elizabeth would like to know if there is anything we can do to help."

"Apprentice must be stuck," John said with a frown, confirming my fears. "There isn't anything Lady Hawthorne would be able to do about that."

"Still, she asked me to check," I said. "It would be unseemly of me to go alone."

John gave me a nod, tied off the horses with a quick knot, and motioned for me to go first. The home was connected to Elizabeth's, so we didn't have to go far. In just a few feet, we were already pushing past neighbors who had gathered to watch the commotion.

"He is only six years old," one of the ladies said, and my heart sank even further. It bothered me that so many people were here—at least a dozen—watching and waiting to see the catastrophe unfold, but I supposed I was no different. I made my way closer to the brick mason and master sweeper, determined to see if there was anything I could do to help. I had no desire to just watch. I knew that in this situation, every second counted.

As we got closer, I heard the clanging of a metal pipe and the banging of boards being slapped together. "John." I reached back and grabbed the arm of Elizabeth's footman. "Hand me your jacket, and go help those men set up the scaffolding. We both know that mere seconds can be the difference between life and death." John gave me a quick nod, already shrugging out of his jacket. He seemed gratified to have something to do.

He rushed over to the other men—some working class and a few residents of the community—as they all worked together to get the brick mason to the height needed to reach the boy who was trapped in the flue just behind the bricks. Just six years old! I was grateful Elizabeth was not here. With a two-year-old boy at home, I knew this was nothing she should see.

I glanced over at the dirty chimney sweep standing off to the side, watching with a bored expression as the other men worked as quickly as they could to extract the boy. A deep-seated resentment toward the man grew inside me, and I made my way to him.

"You aren't going to help?" I asked him. I could hear the anger in my voice, but I didn't care. "You were the one who put the boy in this situation."

The chimney sweep pulled his eyes away from the workers and looked me up and down in contempt. "Chimney's got to be swept. If we didn't do it, people like you would be whining about children dying in fires and such. Now, why don't you run along home? This isn't going to be pretty."

"You have already given up on him?" I asked incredulously. "Is that why you aren't helping?"

"Listen, lady, I do you no disrespect," he said lazily, spitting some black juices about a foot from my skirt. "But nine times out of ten, when these boys get stuck, it's too late. And this boy is new and small. He isn't likely to make it. So once again, if you know what is good for you, just head home and have a nice cup of tea. Have the maid start your fire in your fireplace, and don't worry your pretty little head about the people that make your life possible."

I took a deep breath, astounded by his lack of humanity, let alone his condescension toward me. "If he is so young and new, why did you send him up in the first place?"

"My other boys are too big for this one. Not that it is any of your business." He spat again. "Most chimneys are a brick by a brick and a half, but this one here has a section that is just a brick by a brick. None of my older boys would have fit." The magnitude of his words washed over me, making me feel slightly faint. There was a six-year-old boy trapped in a space so small it took my breath away. The edges of my vision started to blur as I pictured just what it must be like for the poor child. The sweep casually looked up to see the progress the men had made laying the scaffolding. They had finished, and the brick mason was making his way up it.

"How can they do it?" I asked. "Surely the boy was too scared to climb up there."

"Of course they're scared, but somebody's got to do it. That's what I keep telling you, woman." He looked heavenward in exasperation. "I had to start a fire under this one to get him to climb faster. I really should have borrowed a boy that actually knew what he was doing."

I clutched John's jacket firmly to my chest with my left arm. My right hand balled into a tight fist, and my jaw clenched. I shook my head to clear my vision. I had never met a man so contemptible in my life. He noticed the way I had lost control and leaned close enough to my face that I could smell the horrible stink of his tobacco-laced breath. Several of his teeth were black with rot, making the acidic smell even more potent. "You want to hit me? Go right ahead. It would be a pleasure to be struck by such a pretty little one like you."

Without thinking, my hand went back. It was going to be a pleasure for me to strike him. Just before my fist flew, I felt a strong steady hand grab my arm.

"Let me hit him, John!" I cried, pulling against him hard enough that he was forced to place his other hand on my shoulder to keep me still. "I have never met such a vile creature."

"Don't dirty your hands by touching him," William said. His steady voice was just inches from my ear. He tightened his hold on me, and I could feel him willing me to calm down.

The chimney sweep laughed and then sauntered away. I spun to face William, frustrated that he had stopped me from having the satisfaction of leaving a mark on that disgusting man. His coat was missing, and his shirtsleeves were rolled up to his elbows. His forearms were streaked with dirt, and I could see a sheen of sweat on his brow.

"You helped build the scaffolding . . ."

"Yes," William said, dropping his hands from me now that the sweep was no longer near. "My home is just up the street, and when I heard the commotion, I came to help." Both of our eyes went to the exterior of the home. The brick mason was using a hammer and chisel to remove the mortar around the brick. The scaffold shook with every heavy blow. I hoped the men had done a solid job putting it together.

"Will the boy be all right?" I asked William.

"I don't know," William said, his eyes narrowing as he watched the mason work. "There's a chance, if they can get to him in time. I thought I heard whimpering from inside the chimney as we were laying some of the higher boards on the scaffolding. But it doesn't take long for a boy to suffocate with all the soot that comes loose during cleaning."

There was a shout from the brick mason, and everyone on the street turned to look. I saw John rush to climb up one of the two ladders that had been laid over the scaffolding. It only reached two thirds of the way up. From there, he proceeded to climb to the top of the scaffolding to assist the brick mason in lifting the boy out of the small opening that had been created near the roofline in the chimney.

"Go home, Rose," William said, grabbing both of my shoulders and looking me in the eye. "I will call on you later and tell you the outcome. You shouldn't be here to witness it." He let go of my shoulders and rushed over to help. I ignored his advice and watched as the brick mason pulled a limp child out of the side of the chimney.

He looked so small. A boy like that should be playing in a nursery, not climbing chimneys. It was impossible to tell what he looked like. He was so covered in soot, the only color other than black was the red of the gashes on his hands and knees.

The brick mason passed the boy to John, who passed the unmoving boy down to a man standing on the platform below him. William had made it to the top of one of the ladders, and he was next to take the tiny apprentice. William carefully made his way down from the ladder, keeping a tight grip on him. When they reached the ground, William immediately began moving and shaking the boy, his white shirt turning gray and then black. After laying the boy on his side and hitting him a few times, he laid his ear against the boy's back. Everyone was silent as we watched the pair.

"He's breathing!" William shouted, and there was an audible gasp of relief from everyone in the crowd. William continued to work on the boy, rubbing his hands and legs between his hands one at a time. "Someone run for a doctor."

A portly man who was still wearing his fine coat grabbed the shoulder of another man near him. "Run and fetch the doctor. This happened at my home; I will pay for his care." The man hurriedly left.

There was finally a cough from the boy, and his arms and legs started flailing frantically. William placed his arms back around him, taking several blows to his face and arms, until the boy finally began to calm down.

I watched for a few moments and then turned around slowly. There was nothing I could do here, and I knew I should get back to Elizabeth. I looked down and realized I still had John's coat in my hand. He had climbed down and was standing next to William and the boy. I walked the few yards to them and quietly handed John his coat. As I got a closer look at the child, I realized the black soot was not covering his clothing but his skin. The unfortunate child had been forced to climb and clean a flue so small he'd gotten stuck in it completely naked. I immediately pulled John's coat back into my arms, bent down next to William, and threw it over the boy.

"I will buy you another one," I said without looking at John to see his reaction. I hoped I hadn't offended him.

The boy's shivering slowed, and he tried to say something, but his voice was too hoarse, and it came out like a croak.

"Shh," I said, placing my hand on his abdomen. "You can speak later. You need to rest." His panicked eyes calmed slightly at my words and touch until, eventually, his flailing completely stopped.

I stood and looked at John. "Sorry about your coat."

He smiled at me. "The boy needs it more than I do, and it was high time I got a new one. I'm going to hold you to buying me one."

"It will be my pleasure, John. Thank you for all your help."

"I was glad to do it. I have a little one at home . . ." He paused and gave a small cough. "It makes me sick to think of him having to endure something like this."

The doctor arrived, and William apprised him of all that had happened. When it was clear the doctor had everything under control and there was nothing more William could do, he stood. The whole right side of his face was sooty, and his clothing was just as dirty.

"Let's get Miss Davenport home," William said to John. "Then afterward, if you could come to my home, I have a coat you can use until she fulfills her promise to you."

"And the boy? How is he?" I asked William.

"It looks like he is lucky today. The doctor seemed to think he will make a full recovery. Lord Percival has offered to pay for a hospital stay to make sure he gets the care he needs."

"A hospital? Must he stay in a hospital?" I asked, feeling sick to my stomach. I had only ever heard of the dreadful conditions there, having never been allowed to set foot in one.

"John, take Rose home," William said.

How many times must I be told to go home? By now, they must realize I make my way back to Elizabeth's when *I* was ready.

"I'll talk to Lord Percival to see if there isn't anything else to be done about the boy," William said. "Even though a hospital isn't the best place to stay, I certainly don't want him going home with the chimney sweep. It might be his only option." William returned to the doctor and Lord Percival, and John motioned for me to head back toward Elizabeth's home.

This time I followed John's directions, and we walked away from the chaos that still surrounded Lord Percival's residence.

"Couldn't his parents take him?" I asked almost to myself.

"Most likely, he doesn't have any," John said.

I knew that, of course, but I was still in shock over the whole situation, and I hadn't thought it through.

We had walked the few yards to Elizabeth's door when I turned to see William catching up to us at a brisk jog.

"Lord Percival has agreed to let the boy—Adam is his name—stay in the servants' quarters at his home for the next few days, at least until he is well."

"That is good news," I said with a sigh of relief. At least the boy would not have to spend any time in a hospital.

"How did you convince Lord Percival of that?" John asked. "He is free-handed enough with his money, but not many folks are invited to stay at his home."

"Yes, well, he also has a penchant for fine brandy, and I happen to have an 1811 bottle—a gift from the Duke of Manwaring—that I am willing to part with," William said.

John nodded as he made his way to the carriage so he could untie the horses. "That would do it, I suppose."

William and I stood for a moment, watching John go about his work. "If it was a gift from a duke, I am sure it was valuable."

William made a small sound like a cough. "Yes, well, I suppose I could have had Adam stay with me, but I assumed you would want to visit him." He looked at what I thought must be his home, which he either felt I wouldn't be comfortable in or I wasn't invited to. I tried to pick out which one he was eying, but I couldn't be sure.

"I will want to visit Adam. Thank you," I said, not daring to ask the reason he felt I couldn't visit the boy at his townhome. I started up the stairs and then stopped to turn back to William. A thought had been nudging my brain throughout the ordeal as I'd watched William with Adam.

"You would have been a great doctor," I called down to him.

His right hand was on the wrought-iron railing, and one foot was on the first step of Elizabeth's stairs as he looked up at me. "I had almost forgotten about that," William said with a half-smile.

"You don't often wonder about what you could have been?" I asked. "You could be helping people like this all the time."

"Being a doctor and running an estate are both just things one does," he said with a shrug. "Becoming the heir didn't dictate who I have become. I have been able to help a lot of people who rely on Feldstone for their livelihood, and I imagine that is just as fulfilling as helping the sick. I am the same man I would have been regardless of how things turned out."

I thought about how he had thoroughly ignored me after Joseph left, and I wanted to disagree. He changed completely when he became heir.

"I wonder about other things sometimes though," William said. "Some aspects of my life may have turned out differently had I had more freedom." His eyes went to my lips, and for an instant, I thought perhaps he was remembering the morning I came so inappropriately to his chambers. I shook the notion from my head. It must be the lady in the park he was thinking about. If Joseph were still heir, it might not be quite as scandalous for William to marry so far beneath him. That was none of my business though, I reminded myself for the hundredth time.

I gave William and John a parting smile and then finished making my way up the stairs. My hands were still shaking as I gripped the doorknob. I took a few deep breaths. I didn't want to show Elizabeth my distress. If I was calm enough, she might not realize how desperate the situation had been.

CHAPTER 11

Two days later, I was back in the carriage with my mother and father, headed to Feldstone Manor. I had visited Adam both days before we'd left, and he was much improved. He was, by nature, a shy boy and didn't speak much. More than his shyness, his wariness of his surroundings disturbed me. He was completely uncomfortable in such a large residence, even though he spent all his time near the kitchen. Any food he received, he took without question, but until it was completely swallowed, his eyes darted back and forth as if someone was about to take it from him. I hated to think what his life had been like, both in his home and with the sweep. I also hated to leave him for our trip to Feldstone.

It would be a quick stay this time, I reminded myself. We would be there only two nights. It hardly warranted the four-hour carriage ride, but Lady Chatsworth had insisted we have the dinner at their manor and not in London. My pleas of illness had fallen on deaf ears with my mother. If she was going to miss the Tingleys' ball for this dinner, she was certain that I could miss lying in bed to recover. The fact that I had been out of the house so much to see Adam hadn't helped my cause.

As frustrated as I was with my mother, I decided to give her the benefit of the doubt. She had raised five daughters, and although she was not the most loving of mothers, she had stayed with us.

The first time I visited little Adam, I had discovered that he did, indeed, have parents. They had given up on his care and sold him as an apprentice. Even as ill as he had been, they hadn't visited him at Lord Percival's or asked to take over his care. I shuddered at the thought of being truly abandoned.

"Are you cold, Rose? Perhaps you should get farther under the blankets. I don't want you becoming even more ill than you already are," Mother said.

I was cold but not for the reasons my mother was thinking. I slid closer to her and nestled myself deeper into the blankets. "Thank you, Mama, for always taking care of me. I know I have not always been the easiest of children."

Mama looked at me in surprise.

"Of course I should take care of you, Rose! You are my daughter, after all. Can you imagine how it would look if I let you fend completely for yourself?"

"It wouldn't look good at all," I agreed, smiling to myself. She wasn't perfect, but she was there.

As we hit the cobblestone driveway of Feldstone Manor, I was not mentally prepared to face this new situation. Letting go of my childhood fantasies about William and me seemed easier when I was in London. Spending time with Adam had helped me see what real trials looked like. I thought I was ready to greet this new woman without any reservations, but my bravery was quickly disappearing.

"I should probably head straight to my room, Mama. I'm really not feeling well." Perhaps I could stay in my room for a large portion of the visit.

"Nonsense, Rose," my mother said. "You need to greet the family, at least."

I sighed in resignation as the two smirking lions came into view and then grew until we rolled to a stop in from of them. My father exited the carriage, and the coachman helped my mother and me. I drew in a deep breath of fresh air. As much as I didn't want to be here, at least we were out of the dark, stuffy carriage.

A brilliant flash of color from the side garden drew my eye. There was a familiar large feather—no, three large feathers—and garish bows. It was the hat from the milliner's shop. There could not be two such atrocities. Beneath it was the dark-haired woman from the park. I willed my muscles to relax. There was no reason to be upset about this. I needed to be happy for William. He must have told his family about her and somehow convinced his mother to agree to an engagement between the two of them. It was great news.

She was just as beautiful as I remembered her, only now her clothing was impeccable, minus the hat, of course. There was simply no excuse for that hat. Her figure was one that every woman dreamed of, a figure corsets were made for: a tiny waist with curves above and below. She was petite, the kind of woman any man would want to protect and love, not a behemoth who raised seamstresses' eyes and made them adjust their budget for fabric. She turned to look at us, and although she was too far away for me to take in her features, I saw a brilliant flash of white, and I knew she must be smiling. This was the woman William was willing to give up everything for.

I couldn't blame him.

The vision of womanly graces traipsed happily toward a side door, presumably to make herself presentable in order to meet us.

"Rose!" my mother said from the entrance of the manor. I hadn't bothered to move from the spot where I had first landed. "What are you doing standing there? Come. We need to get settled before dinner."

I caught up to my mother. No one from the family welcomed us outside the home on this visit. Perhaps it was due to the cold weather. However, as soon as the butler showed us in, Lady Chatsworth descended the massive double stairway to greet us.

"Sir John, Lady Davenport, Miss Davenport, thank you so much for coming! The men are out of the house but should be returning shortly," Lady Chatsworth said as she motioned to her left, toward the drawing room. My dreams of spending the whole of the visit in my rooms vanished with the simple wave of her hand. "Please, make yourself at home in the drawing room. There is someone here you must meet, and she will be joining us shortly."

A fire was roaring in the hearth of the familiar drawing room. At times, the manor had felt like a second home to me, but suddenly, it felt foreign. All the candles were lit, but it felt dimmer than usual. The bookshelves seemed farther away and the couches more impersonal. I couldn't decide where to wait for the unnamed guest. I started toward Mama, who had found a place on the settee, but realized I didn't want to be near anyone. Father had taken a chair by the fire, and as much as I felt the need for warmth, I didn't want to be near him either. I decided to make my way to the bookshelf at the back of the room. I was halfway there when I realized I wanted to be sitting down and not standing. There were several other chairs to choose from, but I went to the window and sat on the deep windowsill. Hopefully, from there, I would be unnoticed and would not feel the need to speak.

The door opened, and *she* walked in. I had taken note of only her figure up until this point, and I couldn't help but have a selfish desire that her face would somehow be horrible. It wasn't. Her dark hair was pulled masterfully into a neat chignon—Lydia's work. The simplicity of her hairstyle drew attention to her facial features. Her large blue eyes were a startling contrast to her dark hair, and they were framed by lashes so dark and thick they could have been drawn in William's charcoal. Her lips were a perfect rosebud. I suddenly felt dowdy. I had endured a week of irregular sleep and inconsistent appetite. Not only that, I was rumpled and creased from the carriage ride. I was familiar enough with how pale and hollow my face looked when my stomach was this upset to know there was no comparison between this vision in lilac and myself.

"Let me introduce you to my daughter-in-law," Lady Chatsworth said from near the door. Her hand caught the other woman's tenderly.

Daughter-in-law.

There was a roaring in my ears, and I couldn't take in what else Lady Chatsworth said or what was going on around me. This was not a random woman William had decided to introduce to his family. They had already married. I suddenly felt sick to my stomach. Worse than a carriage ride. My hands shook as I gripped the edge of the windowsill. I needed to get out of the room. But first I needed to breathe deeply enough to clear away the dark spots forming on the outer edges of my vision.

The drawing room door opened once again, this time with more force, as if the person coming in was too impatient to let the swing of the door open at its natural rate.

"Look who I have stolen from the nursery!" William said, holding a baby up for all to see. It wasn't a new baby but one who was large enough to be walking. I gripped the windowsill even harder and put my head down. A wife. A baby. William's words from outside his bedchamber rang through my ears. *There is nothing for us in the future; it's impossible.*

Impossible. Because he had a wife and a child.

"Give me my granddaughter," I heard Lady Chatsworth say through the rushing noise in my ears. A strange noise escaped my lips, and I realized it was a laugh. Lady Chatsworth finally had a daughter, and a granddaughter to boot. No wonder she was looking so well.

My strangled laugh caused William to look over at me. I didn't know if he noticed I was there until that moment. He had been too busy showing off his child, his daughter. Deep lines of concern suddenly appeared on his face. He handed the babe over to his mother and started to walk toward me. I curled up in the windowsill, my legs balled up underneath my skirt.

"Rose," he said.

I couldn't help it. At the sound of my Christian name on his lips, I laughed again. I knew I was flirting with a breakdown, and I made myself sit up straighter.

"Has the carriage made you ill?" he asked, worry coloring his voice. His gray eyes examined me up and down, and despite the tenderness I saw in them, I knew what he was seeing: a haggard, wild woman sitting in a window on the brink of doing something insane, someone who would never compare to his beautiful wife.

"I think I might be ill," I said to everyone because I knew there was no other excuse for my behavior. "Please excuse me while I go to my room."

I stood and brushed past William without meeting his eyes again. I couldn't handle the pity I saw there. My vision blurred, and I knew if I didn't get out of the room quickly, angry tears would escape, and then William—kind William, who couldn't handle even letting a small animal suffer—would be forced to find some way to try and help me. It would be much more than I could bear.

I managed a small nod to Lady Chatsworth and Miss—no, Mrs. Flawless—before I stormed out of the room. William had left the door open, so I didn't even have to fumble with the doorknob or wrestle with the heavy door. I looked only at my feet as my pace quickened to a run. *I can spend the rest of the evening in my room,* I chanted to myself. *I am obviously ill; no one will question that. By tomorrow I will have accustomed myself to the situation. In the morning I will make sure there are no traces of my feelings for William.* I wasn't watching where I was going as my whole world seemed like it was behind me. It was a mistake. I crashed into someone.

"Oomph." The man sounded as if I had punched him in the gut, which I essentially had done, but just with my head. I looked up to apologize, expecting to see the butler, but found William instead.

Only it wasn't William. He looked like William, only paunchier and not as well kept. His face was more burnished by the sun. I stepped back and inhaled a large breath.

"Miss Davenport?" William-Who-Was-Not-William asked.

Joseph.

"Lord Tel . . ." I began and then realized my faux pas. He was no longer Lord Telford; William was.

"It is Mr. Lawrence now." He laughed. And it sounded like William. I didn't remember them being so similar. Joseph had always been so much larger than William, and while he was still larger, it was no longer by much. William had slowly grown into a man in front of my eyes, and I hadn't realized how much he looked like his older brother until now.

Everyone in the drawing room must have heard the commotion because most of them filed out to see what was going on. My mother must have stayed on the settee.

"Joseph!" William's angelic wife called out to his brother. She pronounced his name with a strong accent on the last syllable. *She is not English*, I thought with a shock.

"*Estoy bien,*" Joseph replied and then walked over to her and put his arm around her waist. "I am fine," he said in English for everyone else's sake.

I looked in confusion at Joseph's arm wrapped around the woman's waist. Slowly, the world slid into place. It had been Joseph in the park. The beautiful baby girl that William had been holding was Joseph's child. And the woman, whose name I really should learn now, was *Joseph's* wife. The woman he'd given his title up for. I looked over at the two of them together. They seemed so comfortable and secure in each other's arms, and for the first time, I understood why Joseph had given up everything. It was not for her; it was for them.

"But, Miss Davenport?" Lady Chatsworth asked. "Are you all right?"

"Yes, of course," I said and then shook my head as if to clear it. "But I really should go to my room."

William, still with concern written on his face, walked over to me and put my arm through his. "Let me help you to your room."

I jerked away from him. I could see that he was confused and hurt by my reaction to him, but I was still in shock over the whole evening. William wasn't married. He wasn't even meeting with someone clandestinely. It should be fine for him to help me, but I was not quite over my feelings of betrayal, no matter how ridiculous they were. "I'm not a child!" I said, snapping at him as if I were a dog protecting a bone. "I can make it to my room on my own." I took a few clumsy steps while William watched in confusion. "Mr. Lawrence, I am sorry for running into you. Lady Chatsworth, please excuse me for the evening. I am quite certain I will feel well enough tomorrow to visit with everyone, but for tonight, I fear I need some rest."

"Of course, Rose, you are like family. Make yourself at home."

I gave her a nod and headed up the stairs. I could feel everyone's eyes on me as I ascended each step. I knew they were watching me out of concern, but I couldn't help but wish they would all head back into the drawing room. I was quite through with being the center of attention.

CHAPTER 12

No one came to my room to check on me until after dinner, for which I was grateful. It gave me time to process what had happened. William was not married. I had made a fool of myself for no reason. It didn't change anything though. He was still actively looking for a wife, and it wouldn't be me. Which was fine, I reminded myself. I just needed to avoid him from now on. I couldn't keep causing such scenes.

Lydia was the one who came to help me dress for bed. I had hoped Elizabeth would come to check on me when she arrived, but she hadn't.

"Did my sister and her family arrive?" I asked Lydia.

"Oh no, miss, did nobody tell you?" My heart went to my throat as I thought of all the terrible things that may have happened to Elizabeth. "Apparently they started on their way, and your sister became violently ill. They returned immediately to their London home so she could rest."

"No one told me. I haven't seen anyone since this afternoon."

"Really?" she asked. "I heard there was a note for you specifically. After you are ready for bed, I'll find it for you." She helped me into my nightgown and then motioned for me to sit at the vanity so she could undo the pins in my hair.

I sat obediently but didn't have the patience to wait for my letter until my hair was brushed out. "Could you perhaps fetch it for me now? My hair can wait," I said, turning to look at her instead of my wan expression in the mirror.

"Of course, miss."

I couldn't help but fidget as I waited for her to return. Eventually, I started yanking the hairpins out of my hair myself. When they were all gone, I sighed in relief. I grabbed the brush and began pulling it through my hair in quick, brusque strokes. The pain on my scalp was a welcome distraction. Lydia should be back by now. I stood and made my way to the other side of the room. Hoping to see her coming down the hallway, I pulled open the door.

She wasn't there, but William was. He looked as if he had been pacing outside the door, and he turned expectantly at the sound of the creaking hinges. His face fell when he saw that it was me coming out of the room. And then he seemed to take in my appearance. I had not thought to put on my dressing gown over my nightdress, as I was only going to open the door to look for Lydia. My nightgown covered much more of me than any gown I wore, but with just one layer of cotton separating us, it felt as if I were wearing a lot less. My dark hair fell to my waist in brushed but otherwise completely wild and untamed locks. I saw his eyes follow the length of it and then stop at my waist, as if mesmerized. I hastily grabbed my thick mane near the nape of my neck, pulled it to one side, and held it together with both my hands.

My action seemed to wake him from his shock. He gave me a small nod in greeting. It seemed overly formal for the situation. "I was hoping to catch the lady's maid," he said, clearing his throat. He seemed to be having a hard time knowing where to look. He finally settled on a spot just above my head.

"She went to go fetch a letter for me."

"Ah, well. I was only going to ask after you, to see if you had improved at all."

"I am quite well now."

"Yes, I see that." He reddened slightly and once again tried to find a place to focus his eyes. They first went back to my hair, then down the hallway, until finally they rested on mine. "I haven't seen you looking so unwell before," he explained. "I just wanted to make sure you hadn't gotten worse." His eyes held mine fast while he talked, as if he was willing himself to look nowhere else. It made me realize how often he looked elsewhere when talking to me at balls and in drawing rooms. "I will leave you now to rest. I'm happy to see you looking so much better."

"Thank you, William."

His chest rose in one large, slow breath. And then he turned to leave.

"William," I called after him. He stopped, and with one hand clenching the outside of his leg, he turned around.

"What happened at dinner tonight?" I asked. "Has your father softened his position toward your brother?"

He gave me a quiet smile that left me wistful for earlier days. "At first, he was livid. But just like with my mother, little Sophia melted his heart. He tried not to show it, but we all saw how he fell in love with his granddaughter."

"Good. They seem very happy."

"They do." William stepped to the side of the hallway and leaned his back against the wall. I saw his body relax as he looked at the wall across from him instead of in my vicinity. "You know, I have spent the last two years trying so hard not to be like Joseph. I have put my family first and have tried to keep mother as happy as possible. I always told myself that I never could be happy being as selfish as Joseph has been."

"No one can claim that you have been anything but filial," I said, not understanding where he meant to go with this.

His head slid backward and hit the wall behind him. A low curse escaped his lips, and he struck his head slowly against the wall one more time. "Well, apparently I have no idea how to manage my life. Joseph is happy, and I am miserable."

"You have only begun to look for a wife. I am certain you will be able to find someone who can make you as happy as Mrs. Lawrence has made your brother."

He pushed himself off the wall and faced me once again. His eyes looked black in the dim hallway. "But I still couldn't do it, Rose. I couldn't hurt my parents like he did. Even as jealous as I am of his position, even as my heart breaks when I watch with envy the smiles and small touches they share when they think nobody's watching. I see the fruit of their love in that beautiful little girl, and I want it all. This is more heart wrenching than when he left, and I think I might be a terrible person for begrudging him his happiness."

"I believe I have seen the worst of you, William, and even I know you are not a terrible person."

"I wish I could lay with my head in your lap in the garden again." He smiled a sad half-smile. "But we are past that point, aren't we?"

The hall was silent. Some of the smells from dinner still wafted through the air. I tried to think of the food I had missed rather than the pain I had endured for the past week. Thinking he was in love with someone, thinking he was married, and then still knowing he would be married someday. I couldn't handle another moment like that in the garden. It would kill me when the time came to finally let him go. "I can't . . ."

"I know." William gave me a low bow, and when he came up, he was smiling as if he hadn't a care in the world. "I am glad to see you feeling so much better. I hope we have the pleasure of your company at dinner tomorrow night."

"I'm sure you will. Good night, Lord Telford."

He smiled at my use of his title and then stepped forward to take my right hand away from my hair, which I had managed to keep holding throughout the exchange. My hair tumbled loose again, and William placed the briefest of kisses on my knuckles. "Good night, Miss Davenport." His smile was gone when he turned to leave, and I watched him walk away, with my fingers still tingling from his touch.

Lydia returned only a few moments later and found me sitting in front of the mirror. I cleared my throat and smoothed down my nightdress. I hoped my agitation from my conversation with William was not apparent.

"Here you go, miss," she said as soon as she walked through the door.

I grabbed the letter from her and tore it quickly open.

My Sweet Rose,

My hands shake as I write this, for I truly tried to make it as far as I could to be with you at Feldstone Manor for the weekend. I know how desperately you needed my moral support. After our second stop (in only a half hour of travel) so I could be ill, Charles demanded that we return home. I hope you have no fear for me; I am ill for the happiest of reasons, but I am despondent that I will not be able to make it. I will await your return to London with hopes that you were able to bear the time well.

If all else fails, you can hide in your room.

Forever yours,

Elizabeth

My fear melted away as I understood the reason Elizabeth had stayed home. I smiled as I folded the paper and placed it in a drawer in the dresser.

"It seems that your sister must be better."

"Oh, no. She is quite ill." My smile grew broader. I must look like a very wicked sister, indeed.

"Oh," Lydia said, not quite sure how to respond to my statement.

"You must be so busy now that Lady Chatsworth is in need of your services. I am sorry my mother doesn't make arrangements for Johanna to come with me."

"You are only here for a few days; please don't be concerned about me! Mostly, we are all just happy to see Lady Chatsworth so well." She raised her eyebrow as she inspected my wild hair. "I see you have already started on your hair."

"It is wonderful, isn't it? Seeing Lady Chatsworth feeling better, I mean."

"Your hair is magnificent, but yes, Lady Chatsworth's health has made quite a difference in the house. Rooms that haven't been opened for the past two years are finally being aired. There are parties again. Lord Chatsworth is a fine gentleman, but other than inviting your family to come for a hunting visit, he never planned any social visits." Lydia looked truly happy to have the house come alive, even though that must mean more work for all the servants. "Now that Lady Chatsworth is well, I am worried about you, miss. I hear you were quite ill after the carriage ride."

"That's true. Carriages never have settled well with me."

"Yes, but it seemed worse this time."

"Perhaps it was, but I'm feeling much better now."

"It seems you missed an exciting dinner. Lord Chatsworth was not happy at all to have his eldest son return." I had heard this from William, but I couldn't tell Lydia that. "He cheered up eventually though. When he heard the young master say he would be heading to India."

"India? Mr. Lawrence will be moving to India?"

"Yes. Perhaps I shouldn't be saying what we overheard, but I figured your parents were there and you would have been had you not been ill." Lydia looked nervous telling about what had occurred at dinner.

"Surely none of this is secret if they were discussing it at dinner?" I prompted her.

"Well, yes, but still . . ."

"Why would Mr. Lawrence and his family move to India?"

"He is going to try to make a name for himself in the military," she said. "Apparently, Spain didn't work out well for them, and in England, he is too well-known. He doesn't want his wife and daughter to feel the pressures of what he gave up to be with them. He will return to England when he has earned enough to settle somewhere quiet in the English countryside."

"I guess that makes sense," I said, although I couldn't imagine bringing a family on a voyage like that.

"Yes, but Lady Chatsworth seemed to lose some of her spark when the conversation turned this way. I am not sure how well she will handle being separated from her family once again."

"I hope she will be able to handle it, for William's sake."

"We all hope that, but she wasn't able to the first time around." Lydia once again looked guilty about speaking about her employer in such a manner. "If Lord Telford gets married, he will have children of his own soon. Lady Chatsworth will be happy, I am certain."

"I hope you are right."

"If I'm not, Lord Telford will do something to make her happy," Lydia said with a smile. She had great respect for William. Everyone did.

Lydia finished my braid and tied a ribbon to the end of my hair. "Is there anything else I can do for you, miss?"

"No, I just need a good night's sleep. Thank you, Lydia."

She curtsied and made her way to the door. Just before opening it, she turned to me. "Sleep well, Miss Davenport. I am looking forward to making up your hair tomorrow. Don't disappoint me by staying in bed." It sounded like something she probably would have said to Lady Chatsworth before she'd started feeling better.

"You worry about Lady Chatsworth and Mrs. Lawrence. Plan something spectacular for them. I will see if Mother can spare Judith for half an hour tomorrow. Thank you for everything, Lydia." She gave me a nod and a smile and then was out the door.

CHAPTER 13

"*C'EST BEAU!*" I BEAMED AT Mrs. Lawrence. After an uneventful morning, we had been in the drawing room for the past two hours, working on embroidery. My eyes were starting to burn, and my back was stiff from sitting on the unforgiving high-backed chairs.

She blushed at my compliment, and I was struck once again by her beauty.

Mrs. Lawrence's stitching was unparalleled, and I wanted to ask how she had come to have such talent. I had been led to believe she was a rather low-born woman, but having such skills seemed to belie that statement. Unfortunately, I knew almost no Spanish, and although she spoke some French, neither of us was able to speak it well enough to have a serious conversation.

"Mr. Lawrence?" I asked. I hadn't seen the men all day, for which I was grateful, but I was starting to wonder where they had all gone.

Mrs. Lawrence just shrugged her shoulders. Apparently, she didn't know either. She seemed extremely sweet, but pantomime made for an exhausting afternoon, and I was glad when it was time to retire to my room to prepare for dinner. I assumed she felt the same way.

"Mama," I said before leaving the drawing room. "Could you perhaps send Judith to me before dinner? Lydia is already preparing

Lady Chatsworth's hair, and now she needs to help Mrs. Lawrence as well."

"But my hair is getting so much more complicated as I get older. Your hair looks wonderful no matter how you arrange it. In fact, it looks lovely now; no need to change it for dinner."

"Mother! It is in a cap. I will not be wearing a cap to dinner." She hated it when I called her mother.

"Oh, fine. Then I will send Judith after she is done with my hair. But I don't think she is going to appreciate the extra work."

"Thank you, Mama. I'll retire now and see you at dinner." I gave my mother and Mrs. Lawrence a curtsy and quickly made my way to my room.

"I don't see any reason why you should remove to India!" Lady Chatsworth was telling Joseph as dinner began. "There is plenty of room here at the estate. Your family should just remain here." I could see the agitation in her countenance. Some of the bags from earlier had returned under her eyes, and she was nervously pulling at her napkin.

"That's kind of you, Mother, but we need a plan that goes further into the future. I won't be raising my family on my brother's estate. No offense, William."

"None taken, although I hope you know that you would always be welcome here in the home." He eyed his father and then added quietly, "If it were up to me, it would still be yours to inherit."

Lord Chatsworth banged his fist on the table. "Enough, William! We will not be discussing this at the dinner table. We went over it enough this morning. The estate is yours. Joseph could have ten daughters, for all I care. The heir has been changed by law, and there is no recourse for changing it back, not to mention that production has consistently increased by 10 percent since you have taken over."

"Sorry, William," Joseph said in a voice that didn't sound sorry at all. "Father and I agree on this one. Lucinda would never be comfortable keeping up with the social requirements of being married to an earl. And as far as staying, I understand you would be comfortable with us here, but you are planning to marry soon, and I doubt too many wives would agree with the idea of the former heir running amok in her home."

"But, Joseph, India! It is so far away!" Lady Chatsworth continued.

"We will return. We aren't planning on living there forever. If you want more grandchildren around next year, I am afraid that will be up to William." He gave his brother a shove with his shoulder. "How is the bride search going, by the way?" Joseph chuckled as he saw William get instantly uncomfortable.

"Oh, I don't know what is taking him so long," Lady Chatsworth said. "There are plenty of eligible young ladies. He just needs to draw their attention and pick one."

Joseph laughed outright. "If there are so many interested women, why have we seen no evidence of it? Perhaps they have heard about how you spent your school days being teased for drawing rather than wrestling with the other boys."

"His drawing is a real talent," I heard myself say. I had wanted to say it to Joseph so many times when I was younger but hadn't had the confidence. I was no fifteen-year-old now, and I would probably never get another chance to express my feelings to Joseph.

"It is at best a hobby," his father said with a shrug, and I didn't dare contradict him. So much for my bravery. "As silly as it is, I doubt it has anything to do with the ladies dragging their feet."

"What could the problem be, then? I thought we would be beating off women with a stick by now," Lady Chatsworth said in frustration.

"Perhaps we need a young woman's perspective," the earl said. "Miss Davenport, what do you think?" There was a loud clink as my empty fork fell from my hands. "Finding a match shouldn't be a problem at all. You would be happy to make a match with someone as illustrious as my William, wouldn't you?" Lord Chatsworth asked.

I quickly looked away from William, hoping he hadn't noticed my stare. But my eyes were instantly drawn back to him, as were everyone else's. William had been unfortunate enough to have taken a sip of wine just as his father had mentioned me. He was sputtering and coughing while in desperate search for his napkin. He finally found it in his lap, and with great effort, he swallowed hard and regained his composure. I counted myself lucky that all I had done was drop my fork. Fortunately, William's near-death experience at the thought of being tied to me distracted everyone at the table and saved me from having to answer the earl.

When William finally settled down, he placed his napkin back in his lap, cleared his throat, and turned to his father. "Father, what do you mean?" His voice was slightly hoarse from his unfortunate run-in with the wine. "I have known since Joseph—" he began, and then with a look at his mother and Joseph, he rephrased. "I know I owe it to you and Mother to marry whom you choose, and I had never thought Rose would be an option." He lowered his voice. "I specifically remember you saying only the daughter of a peer would do." He looked nervous. His face was pale, and his breathing had still not returned back to normal after his coughing fit.

"Oh, I remember," the earl said. "I said that because I was so upset with what a terrible choice your brother had made. You are smart enough not to make the same mistake as your brother, I assume."

"Reginald!" Lady Chatsworth exclaimed with a pointed look at Mrs. Lawrence.

"She doesn't speak English, my dear," he said, ignoring the fact that his son did. "I wanted to show Joseph how much better you could do. Truthfully, I still expect you to. Even with this ambitious deadline, there will be time to find a woman of good standing, but Miss Davenport?" The earl laughed heartily, and although it was comical to me also, I couldn't help but be defensive. What was so wrong with me that I couldn't even hypothetically be worthy of his precious son? "Why, she is much too young for you! Of course it couldn't be Miss Davenport. How old are you now, young lady? Fifteen?" he asked.

"I am eighteen this last August, my lord."

"Eighteen!" Lady Chatsworth cried from the other end of the table. "Why, that is perfect!" She clapped her hands. "Oh, Reginald,

Rose would be a wonderful choice. It would be so easy. She is practically a daughter already, and I know she would make William happy!"

I wanted to ask her if she had even seen us interact during the past two years. I could make William a lot of things, but happy wasn't one of them. How had our discussion turned to this? I looked at William, willing him to put a stop to the conversation. He couldn't have wanted to hear this any more than I did.

He looked like he was about to speak, but my mother managed to pipe up first. "I am not so sure Rose doesn't already have an agreement with another young gentleman," my mother said, clearing her throat.

"Mama!" I said. I had no agreements, and I was quite confident she knew that.

"Well, Lord Blakeley has shown you remarkable attention of late, and you haven't seemed to mind this year," Mother said.

"Well, if she already has a gentleman, there is no more need to discuss this." Lord Chatsworth's voice was heavy with relief. He must not have been as inclined to join our families as Lady Chatsworth was.

"There is *no* agreement, Mama. Please don't speculate," I told her and everyone else.

"Well, if there is no agreement between Rose and Lord Blakeley, I see no reason why she can't marry William," Lady Chatsworth said.

"Mother . . ." William said calmly. He couldn't like where this conversation was headed. He had told me in plain words that anything between the two of us was impossible. "These are questions I should be asking Rose in private," he said quietly. My eyes flew to his in shock. He seemed calm now, his face guarded in his usual mask of indifference. Apparently, I was the only one now who felt like sputtering and coughing. Perhaps I should take a sip of wine as an excuse. He must have seen my dismay, for he quickly added, "Assuming she will talk to me at all anymore."

Lady Chatsworth smiled at the idea and then happily turned her attention to the soup.

In private.

Why would he need to speak to me about this in private? I knew he was not interested in marriage to me, despite what his mother had said. Perhaps he didn't want to be rude here at the dinner table. William was the kindest person I knew to everyone else but me. He wouldn't want to disappoint them by publicly humiliating me.

I suppose that was kind after all.

As my mother and Lady Chatsworth moved their conversation to the new fashions gaining popularity in London, William and I ate in silence. The overly large dining room felt cavernous and morose. The rest of my dinner tasted bland, and the sound of the cutlery hitting the china was jarring. My father tried several times to engage Lord Chatsworth in conversation, but Lord Chatsworth seemed distracted and favored him only with grunts and one-word answers. It was a relief when the time finally came for the women to leave for the drawing room.

CHAPTER 14

I WAS TOO RESTLESS TO stay with my mother in the drawing room after dinner. I felt a little remorse abandoning Joseph's pretty little wife. It wasn't going to be fun for her to listen to my mother's few words of Spanish spoken as if Mrs. Lawrence were deaf. I hoped Lady Chatsworth would be able to handle the two of them on her own.

I excused myself, fetched my coat, and headed out to the garden for a walk. It was cold enough that I was convinced no one would follow. The roses in the back garden had long ago been pruned, and only the dry branches poked up through the small dusting of snow on the ground. *William hasn't managed to have these bushes pulled out yet,* I thought. And then I remembered that he hadn't pulled the entry roses out; his father had. The number of things I had misjudged William for was beginning to be astounding. I walked over to the dry bushes and inhaled a scent that was no longer there. I'm not sure how long I stayed that way, just breathing in and out the imagined perfume of my namesake, when I heard a familiar crunch of feet on the gravel walkway. How was it that I knew the sound of his footsteps?

"Rose," William said before he reached my spot in the garden. We would definitely need to start being more formal once he found a fiancée. "I thought I might find you here."

My breath caught as I turned to look at him. He hadn't bothered to fasten his coat, and it billowed out behind him as he made his way purposely toward me. The biting wind caught his hair and toyed with it, pulling it this way and that. His eyes were purposeful and resolute. I imagined a surgeon's eyes would have such a sharp focus. In his hand, however, he did not hold a surgical knife but a blush-colored, hothouse rose. Where in the world had he been able to find that?

He stopped a few feet in front of me. "William," I said, wondering how many more chances I would have to call him that. We both just looked at each other. William ran his fingers through his hair and mussed it slightly. I pulled my hands behind my back. It would be highly inappropriate for me to fix it.

"I have something to ask you, and I am not sure how to go about it," he said hesitantly. "I am suddenly overcome with inadequacies and, more than that, regret for the way I have treated you these past two years."

A painful bud seemed to sprout in my chest at his words. It hurt, but it had an edge of hope burning inside it. I couldn't decide if I should remove it from my chest or let it grow. More than anything, though, I felt that I couldn't face it right this moment; whatever William's question—be it a proposal or an entreaty to stay away from him so his mother wouldn't get such ridiculous ideas—I wasn't ready for it. "It is wonderful to see your brother again," I said quickly, hoping to derail whatever it was William had come to talk with me about.

His thick eyebrows pulled together, and eventually he gave a quick nod. "It has been good to have him home, especially for my mother."

"I am surprised at your father. I wouldn't have expected him to let him in the home, let alone buy him a commission as an officer so he could earn a living in India."

"Ah, yes," William said. His features were suddenly schooled into showing no emotion, as if he were trying to hide something from me.

"Oh," I said.

"Oh, what?" he asked, his fingers delicately touching the petals on the flower he'd brought. He was trying to look innocent.

"*You* paid for his commission." He stopped toying with the rose in his hands and gave a shrug.

"That must have cost a fortune."

"The land really has increased in productivity," he said. "In the worst-case scenario, buying that commission means I may not be able to throw money away at White's for a year or two."

"You never have set foot in White's."

"That is not true. I was elected last year, and Father made sure I went."

"Well, you don't gamble money away there."

"How would you presume to know that?"

"Because I know you."

"Do you, Rose?" His eyes seemed cloudy, like a storm was brewing just under the surface. "Do you know why I have followed you here?" he asked. "I think you might, and I am worried that you so obviously wanted to control the topic of conversation. It doesn't bode well for my endeavor that you want to postpone my speaking of it." He sighed. "But I am afraid I cannot postpone speaking. Not now that I finally have hope." He stepped closer to me; we were only inches apart. He still smelled of sandalwood, just as he had outside of his bedroom weeks ago.

"First and foremost, I feel that I have some explaining to do. One of the things I need you to know is that I promised my father after Joseph ran away that I would marry whomever he wished."

"I did hear something like that at dinner." William was to be an earl. I would've been more surprised if they had given him leave to marry whomever he wanted.

"I've wished thousands of times that I never made that promise. But you were here when Joseph left. You saw what it did to my family. I didn't dare add to my parents' worries."

William walked over to the empty rosebushes. He bent over and breathed in their imagined scent just as I had done not long ago. It was a strange thing to do when he held a fresh rose in his hand. He smiled. "You know, even when you are gone, every summer, these roses are still here, goading me with their scent." He straightened and cleared his throat. "Soon after I gave my word that I would marry only according to my parents' wishes, I discovered you would never be a choice. My father made that very clear when he made me heir. He was adamant about me marrying very well for my station. I never in a million years would have imagined that you would have been considered an option." The air left my lungs in a painful rush. Of course he hadn't; William had only ever seen the worst in me, but hearing him say it hurt.

I started back toward the house. I didn't want to hear whatever it was he was going to say next.

He was faster than I. He came up behind me in an instant and grabbed my elbow. I stopped but didn't turn to face him. His hand slid from my elbow to my hand, and he took it in his own. I took one more step forward, but he didn't let go. We stood there like that for a time, my hand behind me, lifted in the air slightly by the pressure of William's hold on it. Feldstone Manor was in my view. If I could get there, I would be safe, it seemed to say.

"After you left the dining room, I couldn't stop thinking about what my mother said. She looked so happy at the thought of a union between us." He paused a moment, and I felt his hand squeeze mine slightly. "She has been so ill, and although she is doing better now, I am afraid unless I am engaged before Joseph leaves, she will be ill again." He cleared his throat. "For this to be the thing that could cure her, it would make me the happiest man on earth. My mother is willing to overlook any inequality in station, and I am hoping you will be able to overlook how utterly abominable I have been to you." Again, a pause during which he inhaled and exhaled deeply as if to fortify himself. "What I am saying, Rose"—his hold on my hand tightened—"I'm wondering if you would have me as a husband?"

I closed my eyes slowly but still did not turn to face him. I was afraid to meet his eye. This couldn't be happening. If I waited long enough, I would wake up, or William would laugh it all off as a joke.

I waited, and so did William. There were no birds outside this time of year, no creatures making noise. The only sounds in the garden were those of the wind and our breathing. He wanted me to answer his question. Perhaps he was serious. I opened my eyes to take in the gardens around me and the massive manor in front of me. I tried to imagine my life here with William. Would we go back to how we were before? Or would he continue to ignore me and insult me, marrying me only for his mother's health? When I didn't answer right away, he tried again, his voice quieter this time. "I need to know, Rose. Even if it is just to please my mother, to help her keep her health, would you have me?"

I lifted my free hand to my mouth and bit down sharply on my forefinger. I needed something to ground me in reality. He didn't want me. The dream of newly planted rosebushes in the front courtyard vanished before it was even fully formed in my mind. I knew William couldn't want this, but he was willing to tolerate me to give his mother back her health. I thought of the old William, my William, and I closed my eyes, trying to remember him as he had been. I had loved him then. He had been my first love. I could admit it to myself now, but I had always known nothing could come of it, even then.

Here was my chance though. Was I willing to marry him, even knowing it was not for love that he asked me but only to restore his mother's health? It scared me to think that I might. "To please your mother," I found myself saying, feeling oddly removed from the situation. "I might be able to do it." I turned to face him now and was startled by how close he was. I slowly pulled my hand out of his grasp. "But I need some time, William. We haven't exactly been on friendly terms lately." He didn't seem satisfied with my answer. His boot traced a pattern in the dirt.

"Do you think we could make a go of it? I mean, we could try harder to get along," he finally said.

I laughed. "Get along? Have you not been here the last two years? We can't even speak to each other without causing pain."

"That was my fault," he said. "You know I wasn't always that way with you."

"But how can I agree to this when I don't which version of you I would be marrying?" Would he be the William of the past? Could we become friends again? Or would I be ignored and be a wife in name only? I noticed his jaw clench. The flower in his hand bent at a funny angle. He had ruined the stem with his iron grip. "Let us see reason," I continued. "You are no longer kindness personified." William's face blanched. When Joseph had called him that, I had thought it was true. For some reason, it had bothered William to be called kind. Joseph had always thought of him as weak. Kindness, together with his drawings, was proof to Joseph that William wasn't much of a man.

"I might have been that once, but not anymore. Is that what you are saying?" His face was darker now but not with the anger I had seen in him at Mrs. Wright's. It looked to me like a deep sadness and despair. I stepped away from him, and his eyes dulled at the movement. "How do I seem to you now, Rose, if, as you say, I am no longer kind?" His voice was oddly even. As if he were trying to show me my answer didn't matter to him. "Am I just a blackguard who says and does whatever he pleases?"

I shook my head in denial. I wanted to retract and start again. I didn't think that terribly of him, and if we really were serious about an engagement, it was time I tried to see more of the good side of William again.

I was too late though. The somber ache in his eyes was unmistakable, no matter how much he tried to disguise it in his voice.

"You would consider engaging yourself to someone you obviously cannot stand for the sake of my mother?" William asked. "Are you certain?" He stepped closer to me and eliminated the space I had created between us. He waited for an answer, but I had none. Instead, we stood there, silence taking over the garden once again.

"You saw her," I finally said, exasperated. "She was finally looking well for the first time since Joseph left. Now that he is leaving again, there are shadows coming back into her eyes."

"And you would be willing to spend your life unhappy to ensure her happiness? That is the most ridiculous thing I have ever heard," he said.

Then why did you even ask me? "But it's exactly what you are doing!" I defended myself.

"No, Rose, it is not!" He shook his head. "Besides, she is *my* mother," he said, placing his fingers on his immense chest. They rose and fell with every forceful breath.

"And you are the only one who can care about your mother? She is important to me too!" I said, starting to get angry myself. What did the man want from me?

"So can I consider us engaged, then?" His question was low and guttural, like a growl. "You care enough about my mother to go through with this?"

I was so taken aback by his question and his tone that I didn't know what to say. He stood there pulling petals off the already broken rose—not one at a time but in large clumps. He wasn't even looking at it. It was as if he didn't even catch what his hands were doing. Perhaps he wanted me to say no. I could give him an out and refuse him. But his eyes didn't only hold anger and sadness; there was also desperation. I knew he would be devastated if his mother retreated to her room again.

Lady Chatsworth had become like a second mother to me, so I understood why he wanted to please her enough to marry someone he would never have thought to otherwise. I didn't think I could disappoint her, and I knew William didn't want to.

"Yes," I said, and the world dropped out from under me as I answered the question.

William's hands stilled, and no more pink petals floated to the ground.

Engaged. It seemed so final.

I stuck my chin out in a poor attempt at bravery. "I suppose you may," I said shakily.

As soon as the words were out of my mouth, he took two large steps to close the distance between us. He dropped the disfigured flower to the ground, put his right hand to the back of my neck, and pressed his forehead against mine. "I'm not sure I believe what I just heard," he murmured. "Say it again, Rose." He whispered my name fiercely, and for the first time, it felt intimate and scandalous, which was ridiculous, as we were now engaged. He could call me whatever he wanted. "Please."

Well, since he had asked so nicely. I felt myself smile and my world settle into place. "Yes, William. You may consider us engaged."

He let out a sigh, and I felt his body relax. "Being near you these past two years . . . seeing you live in my home, eating my dinner, cheering my mother, dancing with other men, sharing the same air, and knowing I could never do this has been the most excruciating thing I have ever had to bear."

The air in the garden seemed to still, the cold wind forgotten as he breathed my name again and stepped even closer to me, pushing me back one step at a time until I bumped into the ancient oak behind me. With nowhere else to go, his body folded into mine. He lifted both of his hands to my cheeks and slowly, ever so slowly, moved his mouth closer to mine. "And now, I am going to do what I want, like the blackguard I have become," he said. His whisper was a threat but a delicious one.

His steely eyes met mine in a dare. I could still step away, he seemed to say, and change my mind, but I had never backed down from one of William's dares, and I wasn't about to start now. I didn't move as he continued his painfully slow descent. Just when I thought our lips would never meet, he closed the last few inches in a swift, hungry movement. I closed my eyes, and all my other senses came alive. I could feel and taste William, and it was intoxicating. I wanted to see his eyes, to see if he was still upset about my earlier words. I didn't have his power of reading minds, but I thought in that moment that perhaps I could figure out what he was thinking. My eyes fluttered open, but any chance of understanding him that way was lost; his eyes were closed. His thick lashes were like a dark crescent moon against his skin. It felt wrong to look at him, so I closed mine as well.

Engaged. The word flashed through my mind; it was enough to stop my second-guessing what was going on and pay attention to what William was doing. His hands slipped from my cheeks to the back of my neck, and his fingers slid into my hair. There were parts of William I wanted to explore, so I reached my hands underneath his heavy coat and grabbed his jacket near the back of his waist, pulling him closer to me.

He stopped moving for a moment, and I wondered if I had breached some sort of etiquette. Manners were forgotten an instant later when he deepened the kiss and I felt my body press even harder into the sturdy oak tree. I needed air, but I wasn't willing to stop this kiss. We would marry, I thought, and then I would get countless kisses, all of his kisses. But something in the back of my mind worried that this would be my only chance to share this with him.

He must have run out of air too, for he broke away from my mouth and inhaled sharply, but he didn't step away. He untangled his fingers from my hair, and they slid down my neck until he held me by the shoulders instead. He seemed to be looking for something in my eyes, and I liked whatever it was he found there, for he kissed each one and then trailed kisses down my cheek until his lips softly brushed the top of my neck, just under my ear. His feathery touch in such a vulnerable spot made me involuntarily gasp. How had I never realized how sensitive my skin was there?

He placed three more delicious kisses on my throat as he made his way to the other side of my neck where he paused to lightly nibble my ear once. I could feel my breath coming faster, and I started to feel lightheaded. My hands slid up William's back so I could hold myself more steadily against him, and just as I did, his lips found mine again. This kiss was different. His lips were firm and demanding. My fingers dug deeper into his jacket. To be wanted by William was inconceivable, and yet it was getting harder to deny it. Slowly, the kiss became tenderer, softer, and more hesitant. I smiled against his lips, and the sensation was exhilarating. Just as I was about to return his kiss, his grip on my shoulders loosened, and his hands slid slowly down my arms until he held each of my hands in his own. With his lips still on mine, he stepped back slightly, and I was no longer wedged between him and the oak. Standing on my own was more difficult than I remembered. I thought about leaning back into the tree, but that would've increased the distance between us.

His mouth separated from mine, and his breathing was as ragged as my own. My body tingled everywhere he had touched me with his hands and lips. My cheeks felt flushed, and I swiftly pulled my hands out of his and put them on my face. I couldn't look at him; everything was too new. I kept my hands over my eyes and cheeks while I waited for my pulse to return to normal.

It never had the chance.

"What the devil is going on here?" Lord Chatsworth said, his voice unmistakable.

William stepped away from me, hastily grabbed one of my hands away from my face, and turned to confront his father. Lord Chatsworth had both hands on his hips, his normally calm visage was red, and veins were protruding from the sides of his neck.

"Nothing untoward has happened, Father. I asked Rose to marry me, and she has agreed."

"I haven't agreed," Lord Chatsworth said. His voice was steely, slow, and deliberate. His eyes, so similar to William's, flashed like a flame just stoked on a fire.

"Mother agreed—no, more than agreed. She seemed to genuinely want this."

"When I made you heir, I made it perfectly clear that you would marry only with *my approval.* A condition you agreed upon." Lord Chatsworth looked me over from head to toe. I instinctively stepped behind William, seeking protection from his father's cold, calculating glance. The shake of his head made it clear that I was unwanted.

"She will not be the next Lady Chatsworth," William's father said.

"If I were you," William said, "I would be less concerned with the future Lady Chatsworth and more concerned with the current one." William took a deep breath, and his chest grew in size. He looked suddenly larger than his father. All of the hours he'd spent working with his tenants had made his body much more powerful than his father's. The leisurely pursuits Lord Chatsworth occupied his time with did nothing to fortify his physique. "What happened here has nothing to do with who Rose is; it is what Mother wants! This marriage will make her happy, and that is reason enough to ignore any other faults Rose may have."

What happened here had nothing to do with me. I closed my eyes for a moment and let William's declaration to his father sink in.

What happened had nothing to do with me.

The faults I may have.

The faults I *must* have. William truly was doing this only for his mother. My many faults had only been overcome because of her. I pulled my hand out of William's grasp. I had thought he cared for me, but it seemed as though, once again, I had been wrong. And now he was about to destroy his relationship with his father over this.

"So you are only doing this to please your mother?" Lord Chatsworth asked.

William nodded. With that small movement of his head, he destroyed the last of my hope.

"That is easily remedied," his father said. "I will go speak to her now."

I stepped out from behind William before Lord Chatsworth could turn to leave. "You have always been a gracious host, Lord Chatsworth," I said. "I'm sorry to have repaid you so despicably." I sensed William's head whip around in alarm, but I didn't dare turn to look at him. "You are perfectly right about Lord Telford and me not being a good match. But we thought if it could make Lady Chatsworth well, maybe we could make do together."

"I can find my son a fiancée within a fortnight. There's no reason to rush into an unsuitable relationship."

"I'm certain you are correct, sir," I said. I was still ignoring William. I couldn't look at him. It was too soon after what I thought had been a life-changing kiss. To keep my pride in any way intact, I needed some of his practiced aloofness.

"But I talked to Mother before coming out here," William said. "She will be expecting it."

"Well then, tell her she refused you," Lord Chatsworth said as if the matter was settled.

"I will not misuse Rose that way."

"Miss Davenport!" his father practically shouted. The veins in his neck popped out alarmingly. "She is Miss Davenport." I shook my head with a low chuckle at the irony. He and my father were the first ones to declare that we should use Christian names. My laugh made both men turn to look at me.

"It's fine, William," I said, reaching out to place one of my hands on his arm. "If your father can find you another bride who will make your mother happy, there is no need for us to marry. Please don't feel entrapped by what just happened. We were both just trying to please your mother. You are welcome to go back to the manor and tell her whatever you want."

William closed his eyes and took a large breath. Instead of filling him up, though, the breath seemed to leave him deflated. What a mess we had made of things.

"Well then, it is all settled," Lord Chatsworth said. "She doesn't want to marry you after all." Actually, I hadn't said that. But no one seemed to notice. "I will go tell your mother."

"No!" William said, and I bit my lip to keep my hope from showing on my face. I didn't want to be the reason William and his father fought, but it was hard to feel that I was so easily thrown over. "Let me talk to Miss Davenport first." His eyes found mine and then went to my lips. I pressed my teeth down harder into the soft flesh. "And then I will be the one to tell Mother." I stopped biting my lip. There was no more hope that needed hiding.

William's father gave him a nod. "I am glad to see I have one son I can trust to do the right thing," Lord Chatsworth said and then turned and walked back toward the house with one hand clasping his other wrist behind his back.

"Rose," William said when his father was out of earshot. I closed my eyes and rolled the sound of my name on his lips around in my head, enjoying it one last time.

"Miss Davenport," I said. It was time for William to be dutiful and obey his father. I slowly opened my eyes and was instantly sorry.

William took no pains to hide his regret; one hand covered most of his face, and the other was clenched into a fist. He was looking down at the dirt by his feet. With a groan, he lifted his other hand to his face and massaged his forehead in rough, angry movements.

"I'm sorry, Miss Davenport," he said when he finally looked at me, and my heart sank even further. "I have compromised you for my own selfish reasons, and it was low, even for me." Anger and remorse enveloped his voice. "I'm going to go back to the house. I will tell my mother you refused me."

I understood him, and I knew that this was our only recourse, but I couldn't speak. I was still processing the fact that William and I were being pushed apart again.

"Thank the heavens you are leaving tomorrow," he said. "You won't want to see me after all that just transpired." He rubbed both of his eyes roughly with his fingers that just a few short minutes ago had been tangled in my hair. "Actually, I should leave tonight. I don't know how I will face you in the morning. I will make something up to tell Mother. Don't worry, Rose. As long as I keep my promise and marry quickly, I am sure her health will keep improving."

He probably told me that to make me feel better.

He turned on his heel and walked swiftly toward the manor.

"William!" I called after him, even though it was shameless of me. I wanted a small token of care from him, perhaps a sentence or two to say that being married to me wouldn't have been the worst thing in the world. He paused, and I counted two breaths as I waited for him to turn around, but he didn't. He didn't even look back but started once again on his errand. "This will break your mother's heart!" It was a desperate attempt to hold on to him, and I shouldn't have used it. The last thing I wanted to do was come between him and his father. But it worked enough to turn him around.

"When it comes to my marriage, it isn't my mother's heart I should be concerned about," he said with slumped shoulders. His father's heart was fine, so he must have meant his own. He was right. Of course he was right. I grabbed the trunk of the tree behind me, and the rough bark cut into the palms of my hands. Perhaps the pain would stop tears from welling up in my eyes. If he didn't love me, then even at the expense of his mother's health, he should find someone he could truly love. Hopefully it would be someone his father would approve of. I gave him a nod of approval, and this time when he left, I didn't try to stop him.

I stayed in the garden longer than I should have, but my only thought was to avoid everyone in that household. When my eyelashes started to frost over, I knew I could put it off no longer. I snuck in the door, careful not to make a sound as I walked into the empty foyer. I didn't see anyone, not even a servant to take my coat. It seemed as though everyone had forgotten I was even here.

I made my way quietly up to my room. Every feature of the home seemed to mock me. *You thought I could be yours?* every tiny piece of stone mosaic on the foyer floor said. *I will belong to another woman, not you*, the dark-stained wood banister said as I made my way up the stairs. I reached my bedroom and realized I would never house a guest here and think with a laugh, *That was my bedroom once, when I was only a guest in this home, not the mistress, not William's wife.* I couldn't handle any more mocking from this home, so I quickly slipped into my nightclothes and fell into bed.

CHAPTER 15

OUR CARRIAGE WAS PACKED, AND after a quiet breakfast, where not a word was breathed about last night's debacle, my family and I headed outside. Lady Chatsworth had not been at breakfast, and neither had William. I hadn't expected William to be there, but I would have liked to see how Lady Chatsworth was faring.

Lord Chatsworth came outside to bid us farewell, and once again, his wife was absent. Surprisingly, William followed his father out. I had assumed he had left the estate already. His head was bowed and his shoulders slumped, and when he finally looked up at me, I noticed his eyes had heavy bags under them. Apparently I hadn't been the only one who had struggled to sleep last night.

I didn't know what I was expecting to feel when I saw him again—embarrassment, anger, loss—but as his boots crunched up the walkway out to our carriage, I was surprised by an overwhelming sense of friendship. William had had a hard night, and so had I. I knew he had wanted to please his mother and marry me, but I also knew he wanted to please his father. I gave him a half-smile, and his head pulled back softly as one of his eyes narrowed with a question. He stopped walking and returned my half-smile with a whole, albeit tentative one. The flash of his white teeth made me feel as though we both would be fine.

He started walking again, but now his shoulders were straighter and his pace not so sluggish.

"Oh, it was such a lovely visit," my mother was saying to Lord Chatsworth. "It was interesting to see the estate in the winter rather than the fall. I noticed my room didn't get quite the amount of sunlight I was used to. It was fine, of course. I can be happy even in circumstances such as those. I will just remember it for next time." She glanced at William and me. Everyone in the household had heard that he had proposed and I had refused him. "If there is to be a next time . . ."

"Certainly," Lord Chatsworth said. "We will have you again sometime soon."

"Oh, well, that is a relief," my mother said. "And with any luck, we won't have Rose with us next time." Mama gave a curtsy and headed to the carriage without looking at either William or me to gauge our reaction to her words.

Lord Chatsworth gave me a nod but said nothing. I tried not to rehearse in my head the words I had heard him say to William and just gave a returning curtsy. It was perfectly understandable that he would want his son to marry someone more prestigious than I.

"Good-bye, Miss Davenport," William said softly. He reached for my hand, and I gave it to him willingly. He held it for a moment, hesitantly, and then lifted it to his lips. My feelings of friendship didn't leave; they grew and blossomed into the desire I had felt for William the night before. He lowered my hand, and I gave his a squeeze. This could be our last intimate time together, and I didn't want it to be burdened with what might have been.

"I didn't see Lady Chatsworth this morning."

Immediately his shoulders slumped once again. "No, she is still in her bed."

"What?"

"She is having a hard time with Joseph leaving, and, well, with us."

My mother was already in the carriage, and Father was about to join her. Without thinking of them, I turned on my heel and started toward the house. I couldn't believe Lady Chatsworth had slunk back to her bed. Did she not see the effect it had on her son?

"Rose?" William called after me, but I ignored him. I was determined to speak to Lady Chatsworth before I left. William followed behind me, but I didn't care. I knew I was about to be impudent to his mother, but I was quite sure my relations with this family were coming to an end one way or another. I might never get this chance again.

I stormed through the foyer and up the stairs to Lady Chatsworth's chambers. I knocked once, a short rap that barely had the chance to echo, before I opened the door.

"Rose?" Lady Chatsworth called in a faint, surprised voice. I ignored her and made my way to the closed drapes and pulled them open with a massive yank. The dim room was suddenly filled with light, and Lady Chatsworth covered her eyes with her hands.

"Lady Chatsworth," I began before I could think better of it. "Your son and I will not marry. I am sorry. I would have loved to have you as a mother-in-law. But matters of the heart should not be pushed in this way!"

Lady Chatsworth sat up slightly in bed, still looking confused. William stood at the door, his handsome face looking back and forth between the two of us, and I couldn't have cared less.

"You need to get out of bed. You have a granddaughter who needs you. Even if she is in India, it will not be permanent, and you will need your health for when she returns." I stopped for a moment to catch my breath before I started into the next thing I knew I had to say. "I know you may find me impertinent, but I feel that I must tell you that what you are doing to William is inexcusable. I understand you feel that you lost Joseph, and that is devastating, but I have watched William these past two years try to do everything he could to please you and to restore your health. He has taken over parts of the estate and improved them in ways no one in the county could have dreamed of two years ago. I know he does this for the sake of the villagers and workers, but I also know he comes here to tell you about them in hopes that you will get out of that bed and take notice of what he has done. He opens your drapes every day so you can have some sunshine. He visits the neighbors you feel need the family's care. He has done all of this as you have lain in your bed and pined after a son who has left you."

"Rose," William said from the doorway. My name was drawn out carefully and calmly, as if he were talking to a skittish horse.

"No, William, I am not done," I replied in a snap, and he backed down. He must have sensed that I was about to burst, and I suddenly felt bad that he had to stand and contend there with two unhinged women. "This marriage idea is absurd, and he has agreed to it because it has been the only thing to get you out of this room and back into life again, but I should think that as a mother, you should see that setting a six-month deadline on a marriage is a dangerous game to play with your son's happiness. You should want what is best for him. You should want what would make him most happy. And I know that right now, that is not a rushed engagement. It is for his mother to have her health back. And that, Lady Chatsworth, is completely in your power."

Lady Chatsworth was sitting up in her bed and gulping for air like a fish pulled from a stream. I hoped I hadn't made her condition worse, but I trusted William to care for anything she needed after I left. I moved away from the window and brushed past William, who was still in the doorway. As my clothing brushed against his, I felt a tiny spark. It made me turn around and say one more thing to his mother.

"William is not Joseph, Lady Chatsworth. His choices in life are going to make you proud. They already should have."

"Rose," William said again as he grabbed my hand. I wanted nothing more than to let him hold it, but I pulled it away.

"You deserve to get what you want, William. At least in this one thing. It isn't in your nature to hurt anyone, but that shouldn't be an excuse for people to take advantage of you." I smiled at him, trying to be braver than I felt. "Take care of your mother, William. I am afraid I have shocked her greatly," I said as I walked away. "Perhaps I will see you in London."

I tried to ignore what I had just done as I made my way back out of the house.

"What in heaven's name did you return to the house for?" my mother blustered when I stepped into the carriage a few moments later. "The carriage is freezing, and you didn't even let us know when you would be back!"

"I wanted to say goodbye to Lady Chatsworth."

"Oh," she said, a bit deflated. "I hope she is well."

"I hope so too," I said.

CHAPTER 16

The next morning, I was dressed and ready early. My visit to Feldstone Manor had prevented me from seeing Adam, and I was anxious to see how he was faring. Mother hated me visiting anyone in servants' quarters, but she didn't go so far as to forbid me from going. Lord Percival was a widower and had been extremely accommodating about letting me come. I rarely saw him, as the House of Lords was in session, but his staff was gracious. I suspected they had all grown to care for Adam as I had.

I knocked on Lord Percival's door, and the butler, Mr. Kimball, answered. When he saw me, his face immediately fell. It was not the greeting I was accustomed to.

"Adam?" I asked. "Has he gotten worse?"

"No, no," Mr. Kimball replied. "He was much better—so much so that the chimney sweep came looking for him."

I walked across the threshold and into the large open foyer of the stylish townhome. "He hasn't taken him!"

"He hasn't," Mr. Kimball said, and I breathed a sigh of relief.

"Then what is the matter?"

"In truth, nothing is wrong. I only feel bad that you won't be able to see Adam."

"Why not? He is well, and the sweep hasn't taken him."

"The sweep hasn't taken him, but he is gone. Yesterday, a gentleman came to the door and offered to pay for him to go to a country school."

"A gentleman? What gentleman?" I asked.

"I am afraid I am not at liberty to say."

William. His name came into my thoughts unbidden. And yet, he was at Feldstone Manor yesterday. It couldn't have been him.

"How did Adam take this news?"

"He was quite happy with the arrangement. I believe seeing the sweep the day before made him quite glad to be receiving an education rather than going back to his apprenticeship."

"I am sure it did," I said, still puzzled over today's turn of events.

"Would you care to come in for some tea?"

"No, thank you. I will go visit with my sister just down the street." Mr. Kimball nodded, and I made my way back to the door. Before he opened it for me, I turned toward him once again. "I truly do thank you for all the care you gave the poor boy. I know he was happy to be here."

Mr. Kimball gave me a nod and then opened the door. "It was a pleasure, miss."

Another ball.

It was amazing that being engaged for a matter of minutes had changed my entire perspective on societal functions. *I should be engaged. I shouldn't be trying to catch the eye of unsuspecting men.* But there I was, two weeks after the broken engagement, dressed to the nines, being introduced to possible matches. For the past few minutes, I had been conversing, if you could call it that, with Mr. Morris. He was a cousin of the host and a complete disappointment.

Mr. Morris was nice enough. At least I assumed he was. I had missed a few of the things he had said to me since his voice never rose above a whisper. I tried not to get distracted by the many other more exciting conversations going on around us. As one of the later balls in my third season, I knew the host was trying to hand me an easy conquest, but I was not sure Mr. Morris knew the first thing about basic conversation.

After our introduction, he hadn't volunteered any information or even asked me any questions. It seemed as though he was incapable of doing anything but answer my questions to him. Our exchange was quickly becoming tedious, so I decided to stop helping him. He shuffled his feet a few times and then pulled at his cravat. I gave him an encouraging smile, hoping he could come up with something to say on his own.

"The weather . . ." he began, and then cleared his throat, "is quite cold."

Brilliant! He does speak.

"It *has* been quite cold. That seems to happen in winter."

"Yes," he said, and I leaned in closer so I could hear him, as his voice was fading. "It was cold last winter."

"Doesn't Miss Davenport look lovely this evening?" I jumped at the sound of William's confident voice behind me. I hadn't seen him since my family had left his home, even though there had been chances to. He hadn't been at any parties lately. This was the first ball since our return, so he must be, once again, searching for a bride.

"Why, yes . . . yes, um, she does," Mr. Morris stumbled as he looked me in the eye for a split second and then looked away.

"Just look at her eyes. The emerald color alone is enough to drive a man to distraction, but the spark in them . . ." William sighed. "What could she be thinking of to make such a spark?"

How to be rid of you.

Would William never leave me alone? He stood straight and tall. His words were never hard to hear, nor was conversation with him ever tedious.

"Um, yes. You're correct. Your eyes, Miss Davenport, are quite . . . green." Mr. Morris was sounding more confident, as if all he'd needed was someone to tell him what to say all along.

"Thank you, Mr. Morris," I said, trying to ignore William. Mr. Morris blushed a deep red at my gratitude.

"Her green eyes, her kindness, and those lovely dark locks of hair." William's eyes traveled down to my waist, and I knew he was remembering the evening outside my chambers. He was purposely trying to make me uncomfortable, and I didn't know why. "Everything about her is soft and good and pleasant, like an evening by a fire, surrounded by friends. The only thing that is hard about Miss Davenport is watching her and knowing other men see it too. Or, they see a portion of it, for I am convinced no one can know and need Miss Davenport as much as I do."

At his mention of needing me, my breath caught, but I remembered the way he'd walked away from me and knew this wasn't some kind of confession. He had to have an ulterior motive. Mr. Morris also noticed the intimacy of William's words, and with a nod to me, he started to shirk away. Poor fellow—he hadn't even mustered up the courage to ask me for a dance.

"What do you want, Lord Telford? If it is to chase away any of my prospects, I believe you have started out well."

"Was he truly a prospect, then? Mr. Morris is a good man, but I would have thought you needed more stimulation than he could provide."

"What gives you the idea that you have any right to advise me in any way regarding suitors?" I could hear the anger rising in my voice, but I was determined not to have him hear it. I took a deep breath in an attempt to calm myself. It was hard when he was so near me and so large. His chest blocked most of my line of sight. "We were friends once, Lord Telford, and I would rather try to remember those times with fondness, but the more you interfere with my life, the more I have to close that part of me off. Please, for the sake of the friendship we once had, just leave me alone."

"Are your feelings that far gone, then?" he asked. "Am I starting from scratch without even our good times to build upon?"

"I have no idea what you can mean."

"I made a mistake in the garden."

My eyes moved to his lips, and I remembered the softness of them. My hand instinctively went to my neck. His touches there had haunted me more than anything else. His eyes followed my movement, and I saw a hint of the terrible regret he showed on that day. It was a good reminder that he didn't feel the same things I did. I quickly removed my hand from my throat. "I believe you have thoroughly apologized and voiced your regret already. I think it best if we both just forget it ever happened."

"Can you?" he asked. "Can you really?"

"I . . . Well, of course I won't be able to totally forget." I paused and blinked my eyes. In the split second they closed, I was in the garden, kissing William. "You completely humiliated me, and humiliation is a hard emotion to leave behind."

"Ah, yes. Humiliation. That is what you felt."

"I can't imagine what else I could have felt in that situation."

"It wasn't at all what I was feeling."

"Oh, yes, I am aware. Your primary emotion was plain to see. The remorse you showed was unmistakable, and it still is. If you are worried that you made it unclear that you lament what happened, trust me, it has been, and is, very apparent."

William groaned quietly and then ran his fingers through his hair. He really should stop doing that in public places. His hair was a disaster now.

"Will you dance with me?" he said in a swift change of subject. "The supper dance: has it been taken?"

"Lord Blakeley has requested the supper dance."

"Again?"

"Again."

"Are you serious about him?" he asked me quietly.

"I honestly don't know."

"That's more than I've heard you say about any man."

"Well, I did agree to marry one once." I couldn't believe I said that. It was always too easy to expose my heart to William. It shouldn't be anymore, but I frustratingly still wanted to confide in him. I knew he didn't want me, and perhaps more importantly, his father didn't want me, and yet somehow, I foolishly wanted him to be the one to comfort me in my heartbreak. I looked around once again to make sure no one could overhear our conversation. There was no one near.

"Whoever he was, he was a fool to not take you up on it."

"At last, here is something we can agree on," I replied.

Our eyes met, and for the hundredth time, I wondered why exactly he'd left me in that garden. The answer was always the same. He could put up with me if it pleased his mother, but without his father's permission, I wasn't worth the damage I would cause.

"Perhaps you could also agree to a dance with me. Is there any dance that is available, or am I too late?" he asked. "I hope I'm not too late."

"After supper, I am free. You may have the after-supper dance."

"Thank you," he said and then took my hand and brushed a kiss on my knuckles. "It will be the highlight of my evening." William walked away.

I tried to tear my eyes off his broad shoulders and well-fitted jacket, but my eyes had a mind of their own. Nothing else in the room was quite as captivating.

Immediately, Miss Harden pounced on him. She was blonde, petite, and the eldest daughter of the Earl of Frampton. He smiled down at her, and her eyes fluttered in a way I had never even tried to master. I pushed my sense of loss to the back of my mind. The sight of William with other women was something I needed to get used to.

My first dance partner, a Mr. Bramy from Somersetshire, was profuse with his compliments, but I was not in the mood to be flattered. Throughout the evening, I tried to catch a glimpse of who William was dancing with. Each time I saw him, he had a different beauty on his arm. It was a relief when, after a few more uninspiring dances, it was finally time for the supper dance with Lord Blakeley. I could speak or not speak with Lord Blakeley as I was used to. His smile was becoming more familiar. It wasn't as dashing as William's, but it was pleasant enough.

And his teeth looked real to me.

After our dance, Lord Blakeley escorted me into supper and sat next to me. William sat across the table from us, and he was flanked on each side by two stout, matronly women.

"It is unfortunate the weather hasn't permitted any rides in the park of late. You were absolutely beautiful sitting in my barouche,"

Lord Blakeley said, and I tore my gaze away from William's stare to respond to him.

"Thank you," I said. "And I would love to see your horses again. They were magnificent."

"Oh, I've sold them. White seems to have gone out of fashion, so I acquired two matching chestnuts. You will be thrilled when you meet them."

"You sold them?" I asked. He had seemed so proud of his animals during our last outing.

"Yes. They were still beautiful in their own right, I suppose, but I like to keep only the best." His smile was self-satisfied. "That is why I'm constantly drawn to you."

"And if my particular kind of beauty also goes out of style?"

"Well then, I suppose I will have to trade you in as well," Lord Blakeley said flippantly and then laughed out loud. I responded with a laugh of my own, but after hearing that he had done just that with his horses, I couldn't help but wonder if perhaps there might be a grain of truth in his joke.

Lord Blakeley sobered and gave a pointed look in William's direction. "That man has a terrible scowl. I wish there were no relations between the two of you."

"I am quite certain the time spent in each other's company will soon diminish," I said, not daring to look at William.

"But he has claimed your next dance?"

"Yes."

"And he asked you himself? No one constrained him to do so?"

"No, believe it or not, the gentleman asked me of his own free will."

"Well, if you ask me, I would say that sounds a lot like he is hoping his contact with you will increase."

"I highly doubt that."

"That is because you are not seeing the face he is making as I talk to you." Lord Blakeley reached for his napkin with his right hand and lifted my chin with his left. He took the napkin and gently dabbed the corner of my lips as if I had some remains of soup there. He held the napkin there much longer than was necessary and then turned to look at William once again. My face was still cupped in his hand, and I watched as he gave William a fierce smile that seemed to portray ownership. I didn't look across the table, but I quickly pulled my face out of his hold.

Lord Blakeley smiled broadly when he looked back at me. He brought his face near my own and whispered. "If looks could kill, this side of the table would have perished from the poisonous glare of your Lord Telford."

"He is not my Lord Telford," I said to him. "Please don't use me in that way ever again. If, as you say, looks could kill, I wonder what my glare could do to you?"

"Excite me, most likely; you are absolutely gorgeous when you are angry."

I clenched my jaw and turned away from the marquis, focusing instead on my supper. I was determined to ignore him for the rest of the meal. I fluttered my eyelids up only once during the rest of the dinner to look at William. He was deep in conversation and smiling at one of the matrons next to him. Lord Blakeley must have been wrong.

After supper and everyone else's conversations were finished, Lord Blakeley pulled my chair back for me, and I stood.

"I do love your glare, but I hope you will not remain angry at me for long," Lord Blakeley said as he took my hand and kissed it.

"I am still quite angry," I said as I pulled my hand from his grasp, "but I am never angry for very long. It is a curse, I suppose."

"So, even your curses are lovely."

I couldn't help it; I rolled my eyes.

"I have had some correspondence from the country school, and your little project Adam is doing well there."

"Lord Blakeley! It was you who paid for his schooling?" I said, placing my hand on the back of the chair I had been sitting on for dinner.

"Yes, well, I had thought to keep it a secret, but I was hoping for some praise from you. I am afraid I am feeling unusually underconfident at the moment. It is not a sensation I am used to, and I want to be rid of it as quickly as possible."

"Well, Lord Blakeley, it seems that you are as kind as you are handsome," I said with a genuine smile. "How is that for flattery?"

"I think to fully understand your praise, I would need to know how handsome you think I am."

I scoffed at him, but his logic was sound. "One compliment wasn't enough?"

"Not from you," he said, stepping closer to me so we were standing only inches apart. His brown eyes were just as intent as they'd been the first time we met this season, behind the potted tree at the Wilmington's ball.

"I believe the next dance is mine," I heard William say from behind me.

"Is that correct?" Lord Blakeley asked me, even though he knew the answer.

"Yes, Lord Telford is quite right. I promised him the next dance."

"Until next time, then," he said, kissing my hand a second time, this time lingering quite a bit longer than necessary.

William took my hand as soon as it was released and walked me out of the ornate dining hall and into the ballroom. "Thank you for agreeing to this dance. At the last ball we were at together, I was certain you had no desire to dance with me at all."

"You know me quite well, William. I *didn't* have any desire to dance with you at the last ball." I had thought he was involved with another woman at the time. I couldn't help the smile that came to my lips as I remembered how wrong I had been.

"Oh," was his disheartened reply. I wanted to let him know my reasons, but really, that wouldn't do any good. William might have had his feelings hurt because I hadn't wanted to dance with him, but with an engagement between the two of us still an impossibility, I didn't feel that an explanation was a wise choice.

The dance began, and I tried not to notice the excitement that tingled at every one of his touches. We held hands for a moment and then let go. His hand was at my waist, and then it was gone.

The dance was just like our relationship: fleeting excitement when he was near, followed by mourning once he was gone.

"You look beautiful this evening," William whispered softly to me at an intricate turn.

"Thank you. It is all part of my plot to make everyone love me."

"Well, it's working," he said, and a soft shiver ran up my spine. We parted ways, and I took the time away from him to return my breathing to normal.

"I hope you are not planning on making a dance with me a common occurrence," I said to him when our hands touched again.

"I rather was hoping to. It is a pleasure to finally dance with you this year after spending two years only watching you dance with other men."

"All you had to do was ask. I would have happily danced with you, William."

"But my father . . ."

"Ah, yes. Your father. Are you certain you will be allowed to dance with me even now?"

We separated again, and while I was standing opposite of him, I saw a look of frustration on his face.

"I don't need his permission to dance with someone," he said as soon as we were close again.

"I'm surprised he hasn't forbidden you from having contact with me at all. He hasn't asked you to be rid of me?"

"Be rid of you . . ." William began, but I was whisked away by the gentleman to my left. It was our turn to march forward. William was left looking even more upset than the last time I'd left him.

The dance was picking up pace as it came to a close. William and I had plenty of chances to touch hands again but not one for private conversation. After the dance ended and we made our final bows to the other couples in our group, William pulled me to the side.

"We both know my father has ordered me to marry someone of high rank, but if I have learned anything from seeing Joseph again, it's that some things are worth risking everything for. For the right woman, I *could* defy my father."

"Oh," I replied, trying to keep my voice steady. So he was willing to defy his father, just not for me.

"No, I don't think you understand—" he started, but Mr. Morris interrupted us.

"I believe I have the honor of the next dance," Mr. Morris said in his slightly-above-whisper voice.

"Yes, I believe you do," I answered with a shaky smile, turning away from William. I was happy to not have to school my emotions any longer.

Mr. Morris held out his hand to me, and I took it. He didn't seem to dare look me in the eye but looked at the top of my hairline. He hadn't been brave enough to actually ask for this dance. His cousin, the host of the evening, had arranged it for him. I was surprised his cousin didn't come claim me for the dance as well.

Everything about dancing with Mr. Morris was awkward. He never spoke, and his dancing was well below average. I purposely did not look through the crowd for William while we danced, but afterward, I did, and to no avail. He was gone. He must have left after our conversation.

CHAPTER 17

After breakfast the next morning, I was not surprised to see Lord Blakeley's roses arrive with a note to say he would be coming for a morning visit. The maid placed the flowers in the drawing room while I read his note in the foyer. He would be arriving soon. I lifted the gauzy skirts of my morning gown and hurried up the stairs to my mother's room to let her know of his arrival. She loved visiting with Lord Blakeley.

I knocked once and then opened the door. "Mama, Lord Blakeley will be here any—" I stopped midsentence as I took in my mother's appearance. She was on her bed, still in her bedclothes. Her cap had been torn from her head. Tears were streaming down her face, and in her hand was a crumpled letter.

"Mama! What has happened?" I asked in complete surprise, looking around the room for any other clues as to what might have happened. I had no memories of my mother being affected like this, even when my sisters had left the home. "Is there a problem? Has something happened to one of my sisters?"

She was so overcome with emotion that she could only wave her hand back and forth and shake her head. She lifted her other hand, the one that contained the letter, and held it out for me. I rushed to the bed and snatched the letter from her hand. I quickly flipped to the last page.

"Mama, this is from Mrs. Jepson. What on earth could she have said that has you so distraught?"

In a strangled voice, she blurted out, "Her daughter is engaged!"

I took a deep breath before answering. "That should be wonderful news. Why are you so upset?"

"Because," she said with a catch in her voice, "she has found herself a marquis!" Mother picked up her cap from off of the bed and began to tear at it. "A marquis!" she repeated to herself.

My shoulders relaxed as I turned back to the front page of the profuse letter. I knew Miss Jepson. She was quite beautiful, but she wasn't necessarily known for her intellect. A name in the letter caught my eye.

"Is Miss Jepson perhaps engaged to Lord Humphreys?" I asked.

"Yes, Lord Humphreys! A marquis!"

"We have established that Miss Jepson is marrying a marquis." I wasn't sure I could handle hearing her say the word *marquis* one more time. Every time she said it, her voice raised a few octaves. Soon I wouldn't be able to understand her at all. "But what I don't understand is why this is so distressing to you. Is it perhaps because Mr. Humphreys is an overtly ridiculous man?" I felt for Miss Jepson but not to the point of tears.

"Rose! Elizabeth has married the best in the family, and even she only bagged an earl."

I looked toward heaven and said a prayer for patience; I had memorized the short verse years ago. I handed the letter back to my mother, and she immediately threw it to the floor.

"I came to tell you Lord Blakeley is coming to call. He should be here any moment."

"Lord Blakeley!" my mother said, sitting up straighter. "He's a marquis."

"Yes, he is, and he can speak without showering unsuspecting victims."

Mother gave me a look as if to say she couldn't understand how we were related, which didn't bother me. I often wondered the same thing.

A rapping sound made its way up to us from the main level. It was a sound we knew well—someone was at the door.

"That must be him now," I said.

"But I am not ready! You will have to meet him on your own," she said with a frown as both of her hands hit the bed. She very much resembled my two-year-old nephew at times. "Actually, perhaps that will be for the best." She visibly perked up, got out of bed, and pushed me over to her mirror. "Pinch your cheeks," she told me. "I have noticed that Lord Blakeley appreciates when you take extra time with your appearance."

I shrugged my mother's hands away. "I will be fine, Mama, but for now, I had better not keep him waiting."

"Good luck, my dear!" my mother called as I left the room.

I walked down the stairs just in time to see the butler closing the door on the drawing room. He must have let Lord Blakeley in already.

I passed the butler at the landing of the stairs.

"You have a gentleman caller in the drawing room," he said.

"Thank you, Mr. Sparrow. I'll go there now," I said as I brushed past him, ignoring the calling card he held out to me.

I threw open the door. "Lord Blakeley! Thank you so much for the lovely roses." For a moment, there was only silence. I took in the room and realized I had made a mistake.

"Ah, so the roses are from Lord Blakeley," William said, turning around. He stood in front of the table that held the flowers Lord Blakeley had sent. "I should have guessed."

William was holding his own roses. He looked down at them once and then held them out to me. "I hope you can find a place for these."

"Of course, Lord Telford," I said, trying to get over my shock of having William here in my drawing room. I looked around the room and was suddenly self-conscious. William had never visited us in our home before. We had always been guests in his. Our drawing room was not shabby in the least—Mother would never have allowed that—but it was much smaller than the one at Feldstone, and for some reason, I felt the difference keenly. "Let me just hand these to the maid. She will find a place for them."

I reached for the roses, but he held them back. "Is he coming here?"

"Lord Blakeley?" I asked, and he gave me a nod. "Yes, he should be here any minute. Perhaps you should go."

"Perhaps I should," he agreed as he finally handed me the roses. They were the same deep-blush color as the ones that used to adorn the entrance to his home. The same color as the first rose he'd ever given me. And most recently, the same color as the one he had destroyed in the garden.

I stepped out of the drawing room and handed them to Johanna. When I came back into the room, William was still there, only now he was sitting on a sofa with both arms sprawled out. His size made the sofa seem ridiculously small.

"I thought you were leaving?"

"Yes, I thought about it but decided to stay."

"You are going to stay? But Lord Blakeley is coming."

"Yes, I know, and like you said, perhaps I should leave. But I find I can't make myself leave so you can spend the morning with another man."

"Another man?" I asked incredulously. What right had he to worry about whom I spent my time with? I would have confronted him about it, but just then, Mr. Sparrow opened the door and led Lord Blakeley into the room.

"Miss Davenport," Lord Blakeley said with a large enough smile that I was quite certain he hadn't noticed the other guest in the room. "It is wonderful to see you."

His eyes scanned the room now, and when they landed on his roses, his smile broadened. However, as he continued to look about him, he noticed William sitting comfortably on the sofa, and his grin disappeared.

"Lord Telford," he said with a slight nod of the head. "What a surprise to see you here."

William stood and walked over to shake Lord Blakeley's hand. "It is not much of a surprise to see you here, I suppose. Rose—excuse me, Miss Davenport—told me you were coming."

Lord Blakeley's jaw clenched when William so casually used my Christian name. He might have made it look like an accident, but I could tell for certain he had done it on purpose to aggravate Lord Blakeley.

"I must excuse Lord Telford. We are old family friends; we practically grew up together. I am afraid at times we forget to be so formal."

"I see that Lord Telford forgets, but I am positive I have never heard you make such a mistake," Lord Blakeley said.

William raised his eyebrow at this, and I felt heat rush to my face. Surely he wouldn't let Lord Blakeley know that I had been the one to insist on using his Christian name for so long.

"Of course," I said quickly before William could contradict me. "I remain the soul of discretion where Lord Telford is concerned. Now, would you like some tea?"

"Yes," they both said simultaneously.

I sighed and gave William a glare. "I will ring for it."

"I do hope your cook has prepared petit fours," William said, and my eyes widened in horror. He wouldn't . . .

"Have you seen *Miss Davenport* eat petit fours? It is quite entertaining," William said.

"I am quite sure we won't be having petit fours," I said between gritted teeth.

"Ah," William said. "Banbury cakes, then. That will do quite as well."

I groaned out loud, and Lord Blakeley stood up from his seat.

"Miss Davenport," Lord Blakeley said. "Perhaps you should ask this young man to leave. He is obviously causing you distress."

"Do you want me to leave?" William asked. "I will if you ask me."

Yes! I wanted to shout, but I couldn't. His eyes seemed to convey the importance of the question, and I couldn't help but wonder what had brought him here.

"Why are you here, Lord Telford? I thought we had said everything that needed to be said at your estate two weeks ago."

"Not *everything* that needed to be said." His eyes were so intense I had a hard time looking away from them. Why couldn't I say no to William when he looked me in the eye?

"Lord Blakeley, would you mind calling a little later? Or perhaps another day, if that works better for you?" I asked without taking my eyes off William.

"Miss Davenport, if I leave now, I am afraid I will not be returning at another point. Are you positive that is what you want?"

I tore my eyes away from William. Lord Blakeley's face was ruddy, and his back was stiff and awkward. He stood next to the settee with one hand clutching the back of it.

"Lord Blakeley, please don't be offended. I will talk to Lord Telford today, and then I am confident he will have no more reason to visit here." I didn't want to irritate him. I didn't want to be rude. But I felt compelled to hear what William had to say.

Lord Blakeley's grip on the settee tightened, and I saw his veins rise on the back of his hand. "I will leave today, but Lord Telford, if I see that you have hurt her in any way or if her glow is dimmed by your presence here as it has been at balls, as well as that day in Hyde Park, I will not forgive you for it."

"Nor should you, Lord Blakeley. Now," William said, clasping his hands together, "I fear the lady has asked you to leave."

Lord Blakeley released the settee, came right up next to me, grabbed my hand, and pressed it to his lips. "I sometimes wonder at your judgment with the company you keep. I can't keep sending away all the questionable characters you collect," he said, and then he stalked out of the room.

"What did he mean about that day in Hyde Park?" William asked as soon as Lord Blakeley left the room. "Are you still meeting with that man as well?"

I rolled my eyes at William. "The reason Lord Blakeley keeps assuming that man is you is because I thought it *was* you. But I was wrong; it was your brother. So please just tell me what it is you want to say. I was unforgivably rude to a good friend to hear what it is, and I will not waste time explaining things that are insignificant."

"Why would seeing Joseph in Hyde Park be distressing to you?"

I had humiliated myself in front of William so many times. I wasn't sure why fate wanted me to be mortified again. I was grateful my mother hadn't managed to pinch my cheeks; they had been aflame one too many times this morning as it was. "I misread the situation. Now, please, William, what is it you needed to talk to me about?"

"Was he with Lucinda?" he asked quietly.

I didn't trust my voice enough to answer him. I could see that once again my heart would be visible enough for William to stomp on it.

"Was he with Lucinda?" he asked again, moving away from the sofa he had been sitting on and coming closer to me. He certainly was persistent in wanting to cause me distress.

"Why are you acting this way?" My frustration finally gave me a voice. "What are you even doing? Dancing with me, coming to call! Can't you just leave me alone? Haven't you done enough?" I could handle not being engaged to William; I had never thought it would actually happen. But I couldn't handle almost being engaged to him and then continuing on as if we were friends.

"After you left Feldstone, I missed you, Rose. And now that I am near you again, I still miss you. I miss you the most when you are right there next to me but forever out of my reach."

"William." I could hear a tremor in my voice, but I hoped William couldn't. "Please try not to say things that are just going to confuse me. I thought everything was settled between us."

"That is what I am trying to say. And perhaps I am rushing again, but I don't like how we have settled things." He stopped inching forward just a few breaths away from me.

"What does that even mean? Please stop speaking in riddles!" I said, wishing he were farther away.

"It means I am trying to court you!" His voice rose in frustration to match my own. "I am sorry if my skills are so lacking that you weren't able to notice." His hands dropped to his side.

"But why?" I asked. There could be no possible reason why.

"I know I rushed you at Feldstone. I had never even asked you to dance. I can hardly count Elizabeth's meddling as an invitation from me. And yet, I was hoping after that bumbling proposal in the garden that you would agree to marry me? I realize now that I was too hurried. I should have taken my time, tried to make you fall in love with me."

"Why are you so bent on me falling in love with you?" My hands were curled up like claws at my waist. "Haven't you caused me pain enough?"

"I am not trying to cause you pain. I want to marry you! Before you left the manor, you were the one who told me I deserve to get what I want. It's you, Rose. Having you with me for the rest of my life is the one thing I want." His eyes were fervent, but so had they been at Feldstone just before he'd kissed me. All it had taken was one word from his father, and it had become apparent it had all been an act to please his mother. I didn't dare let my heart hope that he might mean what he was saying.

"Did your mother tell you to do this?" I asked. It was the only thing I could think of that would explain his change of heart.

He walked away from me and over to the dark-oak credenza at the side of the room. He rubbed the side of it with his fingertips, hesitant to answer my question. With his eyes on his hands, he said, "I worry that if I answer that, you will misunderstand."

"So she did." I steeled my heart against him, grateful I hadn't allowed myself to fall once again into his trap.

"Well, yes," he admitted. "When I told her that you refused me, she did say I should try courting you in earnest to see if I could get you to change your mind."

"But I didn't refuse you, did I, William?" Every time I got closer to him, he hurt me, and I couldn't let that happen again. I knew his father didn't actually approve of me as a wife, so even if this could make his mother happy, I wasn't sure William would want to go against his father's wishes. "Let's go over what happened at Feldstone, shall we? You accosted me and left me there, feeling like I had been used. I agreed to marry you, which must not have been something you truly wanted, for you certainly escaped that situation as soon as your father gave you an out. I cannot take any more of this confusion. I need you out of my life, William. I need you to go."

"You're right," he said, looking empty. "Of course you are right. I'll go." I bit my lip, waiting for him to leave me once again. At least this time it was of my own doing. He didn't though. He watched me. And when he started to move, instead of making his way to the door, he came back to my side. I felt an angry tear slip from the corner of my eye, and he reached up to wipe it away with his thumb. "I am so sorry, Rose. Miss Davenport," he corrected himself. "I didn't mean it."

"I know you didn't mean it!" I said, stomping my foot like a three-year-old. "Trust me, I know you didn't mean it." His hand was still on my cheek, and he lifted the other to my other cheek. "What do you want now?" I asked, frustrated that he was still in the room, that he was touching me. I didn't have the strength to tell him to leave again. "Do you want to pretend we are engaged again?"

William dropped his hands. "No, I don't want to *pretend* to be engaged again," he said with disgust.

"Good," I replied. I grabbed both sides of his face and kissed him. Because he shouldn't be the only one who got to drive the other to the brink of insanity, and because I was starting to forget what his lips tasted like.

For a second, he stood completely still, and I didn't care. I kissed him with all the pent-up anger I felt at our situation. I knew he didn't want this. He had said as much when he'd said he didn't want to pretend to be engaged. My lips were hard against his soft ones, and I molded them to mine with my head tilted first to the left and then the right. I put my hands behind his head and grabbed two fistfuls of hair and pulled him even more forcefully toward me. I heard a clink and felt the sweet pain of our teeth hitting together. *What am I doing? I can't be kissing William.* I started to loosen my grip on his hair when his hands came to my waist and he pulled me closer to him. He wrapped his arms around me slowly but forcefully. The strength of his embrace caused my feet to lift slightly off the floor. It was as if he was afraid of losing me, as if he never wanted to let me go. It wasn't true though, and I didn't want to start believing it, so I quickly pushed away from him.

"There," I retorted, hoping my voice sounded unaffected. "Now we have both kissed the other one when they didn't want it." I tried to catch my breath and prayed William would not see through my deception. I *had* wanted that kiss. But he could never know it.

Instead of being upset, William laughed. "Did I act at all like I didn't want that? If this is how you would like to be convinced that I am serious in my intentions, I am happy to oblige." He stepped forward with a smile of anticipation on his face.

I stepped away from him. "No! Any time we get closer, any time you make me feel that you might actually care for me, you hurt me immediately thereafter. I've had enough, William. This all needs to stop. Or . . . or . . . I am going to tell your mother I didn't refuse you."

"Sorry?" William stopped midstep, furrowed his heavy eyebrows, and pursed his swollen lips. "You want this all to stop, so you are going to tell my mother you didn't refuse me?"

"Yes."

"I don't see how that will further your cause to get away from me."

"She will have to see, then, that you didn't want me after all. She'll realize you only asked me out of an obligation to her. Once that is cleared up, you will be free to pursue other women before your time limit is up."

"What in the world makes you think I want to pursue other women?"

"You have to if you are going to keep your promise to your mother. I know it would be easiest just to make the first person you proposed to marry you, but that is not going to happen. Your father would never allow it, so the sooner you move on, the better."

I could see that William was mulling over what I'd said. At last, he seemed to decide that my plan to convince his mother to let him look elsewhere might work. "So, you will find my mother and tell her how I was the one who didn't want to marry you?"

"Yes."

"But Mother is still at Feldstone, and you hate carriage rides."

For a moment, I was surprised that he knew that about me, but then I remembered my last trip to Feldstone. I had been quite ill. It would have been hard to miss.

"I have managed to make the trek every year, even twice this year."

"How will you even get there?" he asked.

"If my mother won't part with her carriage, I can hire one. I'll bring Johanna as a companion," I said, proud of myself for coming up with a plan so quickly.

"Bring your maid, and I'll take you in my carriage," he said. "I'm very interested to see how this conversation plays out."

"You can't go there!"

"Why not? It's my home."

"You will explain it to your mother in a way that puts you in a good light. I want her to see the fruitlessness of our situation. I don't want you trying to make it seem like all you will have to do is pay me a few compliments and I will agree a second time and that your father will approve. I don't know if you remember, but your resistance to a union was very apparent the last time we kissed."

"Last time we kissed?" he asked, indicating the spot where we'd been standing just moments ago.

Why was it so blasted hot in here? I wanted to fan my face but didn't allow myself the luxury. He was right. He hadn't seemed to mind my last kiss. "I meant the kiss before that one," I said.

"I can't begin to tell you how much it pleases me that we have shared enough kisses for them to be confused." His smile was maddening.

"That is not the point! The point is, I know you are only doing this to please your mother, and if she knew you didn't want it, she wouldn't force you to marry me."

"So you need to go tell her because I am too afraid to do it myself?"

I threw my hands in the air. "Apparently!"

"All right, Rose, we'll go see my mother. You can tell her it is my fault we are not engaged, and then I will be free to pursue the woman of my dreams." He seemed absolutely happy about this arrangement.

"And no speaking to your mother until I have explained everything to her."

"I won't speak to her until after you have said your piece. I promise."

"I am not sure I want you to speak to *me* until I am able to talk to her." I had come so close to believing William again, I didn't know how I would handle it if he asked to court me even one more time. He gave me a strange look but didn't answer. It was as if he was waiting for me to explain that particular request. But I just stood there, looking him in the eye, while I waited for him to agree.

"Fine," he said. "We will take my carriage, and I won't talk to you for the whole of the ride. Four hours spent in your company only looking at you. I can think of worse fates."

"Eight hours," I said. "If you are taking me to Feldstone, you must also return me."

"What? Today? You should pack for an overnight stay. There is no way my mother would let you get away with such a short visit."

"I am quite certain that after our last encounter, she won't be able to get rid of me fast enough," I said, remembering how I had left her struggling for air in her bedroom.

"I never thanked you for that, by the way," William said.

"For what? Being impertinent to your mother?" I was exasperated.

William smiled at the memory of it. "You were fantastic. I think you shocked Mother into health, if that is possible."

"She is better?"

"She's much better, although she has been doting on me a bit, which has taken some getting used to."

I wanted to hear more. I wanted to know everything about William and his family, which was why I didn't ask any more questions. I needed to wean myself from his life. "I had better round up Johanna and let her know she is finally going to see Feldstone Manor after all," I said, trying to ignore the fact that what I was about to do might lead Lady Chatsworth back to her bed. She wasn't going to be happy to hear that William was the one who didn't want an engagement.

Lord Blakeley had left the door to the drawing room open, and I walked out of the room, and William followed me.

We stood there together in silence while we waited for Mr. Sparrow to bring William's things. I could have left, but instead, I waited as he put on his coat and hat. William thanked our butler and then turned to me.

"I hope you find our trip to Feldstone enlightening. I'll be back within the hour, and then we can start on our silent journey." William gave me a wink and a tip of his hat, then Mr. Sparrow opened the door for him, and he left.

There was a rap at the door only moments after it closed. I had gone halfway up the stairs to find Johanna, but I paused to see who it was. Perhaps William had forgotten something. Mr. Sparrow opened it, and to my surprise, Lord Blakeley was standing there. He impatiently handed my butler his coat and hat and walked into the drawing room without being invited.

I followed him in, wondering what this could be about. An hour was not long to prepare for a trip to Kent. I hoped that whatever he needed from me would be quick.

"Won't you please sit?" I asked.

His pacing back and forth between the fireplace and settee was unsettling.

"Is your acquaintance with that man severed, then?" he asked brusquely.

"I have every reason to believe it will be by this evening."

"Why not this morning? Couldn't you have just told him now to never see you again?"

"I don't think I will need to go to the lengths of telling him that. Our families are close friends."

"So I hear." He sat and quit his pacing.

"Will you go for a ride with me in Hyde Park this afternoon?"

"I cannot."

"Cannot? Or will not?

"I cannot. I won't be at home," I said.

"Where will you be going?"

I didn't answer. How could I tell him that I was going to visit William's mother? He would never understand.

"Where will you be going?" he asked a second time. No longer comfortable on the sofa, he stood and walked closer to me. He was livid, and a spot of fear rose up in my chest. I had never seen Lord Blakeley angry, and I suddenly felt that it would be better for me if I never did. He kept walking toward me until his face was only inches from mine. I was tempted to step back but, instead, decided to hold my ground. "Where the devil will you be going, woman?" His voice rose to a shout, and I looked toward the door, thankful that it was still slightly ajar. If Mr. Sparrow was nearby, he would come in to interrupt any minute.

"I will be traveling to Feldstone Manor, in Kent."

"Which is—?" he asked with his face still entirely too close to mine.

"Which is Lord Telford's parents' estate."

He stepped away from me and gave me a nod. My shoulders relaxed, and I breathed easier with the distance.

"Well, I have no qualms about telling someone *I* will never see them again." He walked to the drawing room door. As he crossed the threshold, he turned. "You are going to have to find someone else to pay for that sooty boy's school. I only did it to keep him away from you."

"What do you mean?"

"You were spending far too much time with the boy. Do you know what that looks like?"

"Perhaps it looks like I cared about him."

"Exactly. It was sweet of you, I'm sure, but there was no need to get your hands dirty caring for him personally. It makes you dirty by association. It was only a matter of time until the *ton* started talking about it."

"Why should it matter to me what the *ton* is saying about it?" This time it was my voice that was raised.

Lord Blakeley looked at me as if he had never met me before.

I assumed I was looking the same way at him. Suddenly deflated, I felt no inclination to try to smooth anything over with him anymore. "Mr. Sparrow," I called out, rushing past Lord Blakeley and yelling up the stairs. It was easier to breathe once I was out of the drawing room. A moment later, Mr. Sparrow emerged from the upstairs hallway and hurriedly descended the stairs. "Lord Blakeley is in need of his coat and hat," I told him.

Mr. Sparrow hurried to get them while we stood awkwardly silent. When Mr. Sparrow returned, Lord Blakeley slammed his hat onto his head, and without waiting for Mr. Sparrow, he opened the door himself and stormed out of the house without saying another word.

"Sorry to take so long, miss." Mr. Sparrow looked sheepish about being remiss in his duties. "Your mother gave me specific instructions that if Lord Blakeley called on you, I should give you complete privacy."

"Yes, well, you may inform my mother that Lord Blakeley will not be calling again, so no such instructions are necessary." He nodded. "And while you are speaking to her, will you tell her that I am going to make a one-day trip to Feldstone Manor? I need to find Johanna and ask her to accompany me." I would deal with William first and pick up the pieces Lord Blakeley had scattered afterward. I had already made tentative plans for Adam before he'd swooped in and sent him out of town. I had a good idea of a family who could help him, and a trip to Feldstone would be the perfect opportunity to ask them.

CHAPTER 18

JOHANNA AND I WERE A flurry of activity, preparing for the ride to Feldstone. My room was covered in discarded clothing and hair ribbons.

"Are you certain we shouldn't pack for an overnight stay? It is such a long ride."

"Yes," I said as she fastened the buttons on my traveling dress. Nothing would keep me at Feldstone Manor longer than I wanted to stay.

"What if the weather becomes too severe to travel, or a horse needs attention?" Johanna asked. That gave me pause. It would be quite uncomfortable if we were caught completely unprepared.

"I hadn't thought of that. I *would* hate for us to need clothing and not have it ready. Perhaps we should pack an overnight trunk on the off chance something happens."

Johanna smiled broadly. She was obviously happy with the thought of staying a night in the countryside.

"If all goes as planned, we won't need it," I reiterated.

"Yes, miss," she answered, but she was still smiling.

William had a matching smile when he arrived exactly one hour later and saw my trunk.

"Oh, remove that broad grin from your face," I said. "We are only bringing the trunk in case of emergencies."

William tried to stop smiling, and he succeeded for the most part. However, as he watched the footman load the trunk onto the back of the carriage, I noticed the corners of his lips sneak up again.

After everything was situated to William's satisfaction, I settled myself in the carriage and motioned for Johanna to sit next to me. Ever since William had arrived, I'd noticed Johanna sizing him up. As he entered the carriage, she looked him up and down unabashedly.

"You never told me how handsome Lord Telford is," she whispered in my ear.

"I guess I never noticed," I lied with a shrug.

William noticed our whispers and raised an eyebrow at me in question. He must know Johanna was commenting on his appearance. Her appraising glances were anything but discreet. As handsome as he was, whispers among ladies must have been a constant annoyance to him.

"You have something on your face," I said, motioning with my hand on my cheek in explanation.

He laughed, a low rumbling sound that started deep in his belly. Not once did he reach to wipe off any nonexistent dirt. I should have known better than to try to misdirect him. He always had been able to read my thoughts.

"Johanna, isn't it?" William said, addressing my maid. She looked up at him with a start, a blush already forming along her neck. "I am not allowed to converse with your mistress, but I must compliment you on how well you have done as a lady's maid in getting her ready. She looks absolutely stunning."

"Thank you, Lord Telford, although I must admit it is easy to make Miss Davenport presentable."

I gave Johanna a nudge on her shoulder, and she looked at me, surprised. "Please don't encourage him," I said into her ear.

"Pardon me, miss," she said, scooting farther down in her seat. Then sotto voce, she added to me alone, "But I really do think *someone* should." After she looked away from me, she fluttered her eyelids at

William, and he responded with a pleasant, encouraging smile that brought out the crinkles next to his eyes.

I took a deep breath. This was going to be a very long carriage ride.

"So, tell me, Johanna, does Miss Davenport ever command you not to speak to her, or does she save such treatment for me?"

Johanna sat back up in her seat. "As far as I know, you are the only one."

"Hmm," William said, putting his hand on his chin. "I am trying to decide whether that is an honor or a bad omen."

"Based on how many times she had me redo her hair, I would consider it an honor," Johanna said.

"Johanna!" I hissed. "Was I wrong to assume you value your job?"

"Sorry, miss," she said quickly.

"We can find other things to talk about," William said to her, "even though I am quite sure your position is safe enough. I doubt Rose will punish you for my indiscretions."

Johanna quirked an eyebrow in my direction when she heard him call me by my given name. "Could you perhaps tell me about Feldstone?" she asked.

William went into great detail telling Johanna about the estate. He mentioned the apple tree and how we used to pluck apples from it. He talked of the bridge with family names carved into stone. "Someday my name will be there, as well as my family's names," he said with a palpable wistfulness. After an hour, Johanna finally seemed to tire of the novelty of a young and handsome gentleman conversing with her and fell asleep. Her head tottered back and forth a few times, then came to rest on my shoulder. I knew she would be embarrassed by it when she woke up, but I let her be. I had assumed the ride would improve once William had no one to speak to, but it didn't. He wasn't allowed to speak to me, but I should have also forbidden his looking in my general direction.

His eyes found mine every few minutes and always contained a mysterious glint, as if he knew something good was coming. I couldn't break my own rules and ask him what he was thinking about, so I just stared right back at him. I'm positive my eyes showed something more melancholy. To me, it felt as if something good was about to come to an end.

I eventually just closed my eyes and ignored him, and it wasn't long before I fell asleep. After what must have been hours of fitful sleep, I awoke to a loud thumping. Johanna jerked to a sitting position, and we both looked around the carriage in alarm. William lifted his gloved hand to the ceiling of the carriage and banged his fist to it two more times. The carriage immediately began to slow.

"Sorry to wake you," William said to Johanna. "You may inform your mistress that I am stopping here," William said. "We are nearly to Feldstone, and I have one errand to attend to before meeting you there."

"You are leaving me to go on alone?" I asked in shock. He looked at me and, in a mocking way, mimed with his hands the message that he couldn't answer my question.

"Let's just be done being ridiculous, shall we?" I asked, ignoring the fact that I was the one who had insisted on such foolish rules. "You may speak to me."

William let out a huge burst of air as if he had been holding it throughout the carriage ride. "Thank you," he said. "I'm stopping here because this is the nearest point on the road that passes by the Wrights' home, and they have an item I have entrusted them with. I am simply going to retrieve it, and then I'll head back to the manor. I'll only be a few minutes behind you. As I recall, you wanted to talk to my mother before I could anyway."

"But I haven't an invitation to your home. How will I get in?" I asked.

"I imagine Howard will let you in, assuming he can still open the front door. That door will probably outlast the stonework on the building." He tipped his hat to us both and then swung the carriage door open and jumped out.

"Wait! William, I have something I need to discuss with the Wrights. Perhaps I should come with you."

"Sorry, Rose, you need to talk to my mother first. I can't let you see my errand here," William said.

"But I don't know if I will have another chance to see them on this trip."

"Perhaps I could relay a message for you." William's hand was on the carriage door as he waited for my reply. I really would have liked to make my supplication in person. But I knew he cared about Adam as much as I did, and there really wouldn't be much time to stop on the way home.

"I wanted to ask them about Adam."

"Isn't he at a school in Suffolk?"

"He is, but I want to bring him here." William's eyebrow rose, and I realized my presumption. I had nothing to do with this estate. "I mean, to the Wrights'. I thought they might be willing to take him in. In a few years, I am sure he could provide valuable help on the farm."

"I will ask them for you. This would be a better place for him than a boarding school, especially at his age." It definitely would, especially since his support was about to be withdrawn, but I didn't mention that to William.

"Thank you, William."

He gave me a nod and shut the carriage door softly. "I'll see you at Feldstone," he said, waving his hat as he walked a few steps backward, away from the carriage. His long legs would make short work of the journey, and then I would need to face him again. As bad as this journey had been, the ride home was going to be even worse.

"I am so happy to finally see Feldstone Manor!" Johanna said, and I tore my eyes away from William's retreating back. "I have heard so much about it; it will be like visiting a long-lost relative," Johanna declared. She had made similar declarations to William throughout the first hour of the journey, and now that we were nearing the estate, she seemed to feel the need to repeatedly let me know how much she had anticipated the view of Feldstone. It was too bad Johanna had never had the chance to come with us during Michaelmas. By all rights, she should have been there as my lady's maid.

"Thank you again for coming with me on such short notice and for such a short trip. I am afraid we will not be there long. Just long enough for me to speak with Lady Chatsworth and have the horses rest. I would hate for the two of us to have to stay at an inn." I shuddered and absentmindedly scratched my arm. The thought of staying in a bed at an inn was much more sickening than a carriage ride.

I took a deep breath and rehearsed in my mind what I needed to do. The last time I had seen Lady Chatsworth, I had treated her most abominably, and here I was about to do it again. I couldn't help but feel that I was using her as a way to keep William away from me. She was so delicate I wondered what the shock of finding out what William and her husband had done in the garden would do to her.

My words really could hurt William's mother, which was quite possibly the worst thing I could do to him, but I was tired of being the victim of William's decisions. I wanted Lady Chatsworth to know that I had seen the honor it would have been to marry into their family and how delighted I would have been to have her as a mother-in-law. It was her son who didn't want that.

"Oh! It is beautiful!" Johanna exclaimed as Feldstone came into view, with its hard lines and wild forests. My breath caught as it always did, but this time, it was even more poignant knowing it would be my last visit.

"It is, isn't it?" I said. "Beautiful in a fearsome way. If strength could be beauty, I feel Feldstone would be the most sought-after estate in England."

I hadn't ever arrived at an estate without having a proper invitation before, and I was not quite sure how it was supposed to be done. As the carriage rolled to a stop and we descended, I decided that the only thing to do was knock and hope for the best.

"It won't do for me to go through the front," Johanna said. "I will find the back entrance and see about asking the cook to prepare some tea for you. It will be a long carriage ride back, and you will need some sustenance before we leave."

I nodded, glad that at least one of us knew what to do. I watched Johanna as she found her way around the house. A stableman noticed our arrival and came to offer the coachman some assistance. Everyone else knew what they should be doing. I took a deep breath and started on my task. The first step was to get into the home.

I rapped loudly at the door and waited for it to open. The door was so large and heavy, it seemed to be set there to keep people out, not let them in.

Eventually, I heard Mr. Howard, the butler, pulling the door slowly open with all of his might. His eyes widened at the sight of me standing outside the door, but he hid his surprise quickly. "Miss Davenport, will you please come in?" he asked. I stepped over the threshold and into the foyer that, up until this morning, I had been certain I would never see again. "Perhaps you could wait in the drawing room while I inform Lady Chatsworth of your arrival."

"Thank you, Mr. Howard."

"Will you be staying for some time?" he asked, most likely concerned that they had made no preparations for overnight guests. Poor man. How could they have when I had given them no notice?

"No, I am just here for a short visit. My maid and I will be leaving this afternoon."

He gave me a nod and then backed out of the room. I walked over to the fireplace to try to get warm. The carriage had been frigid, and I wanted to be completely warmed over before I had to get back in it to go home.

My ears were tuned to any sound in the house. I knew that at any moment I would hear Lady Chatsworth's steps and I would have to face her for the first time since I had been completely discourteous to her. I rubbed my hands nervously in front of the fire. Hopefully, she had forgiven me.

I didn't hear her steps, but I did hear the doorknob turn. I swiftly turned to face the door, and Lady Chatsworth entered the room. She had gotten here fast enough that I knew she must not have been in bed. Her face showed surprise at my being here, but luckily, I saw nothing of the contempt I was positive she would feel toward me.

"Lady Chatsworth, thank you for meeting with me, even though I didn't think to send word that I was coming. I am afraid there wasn't time for it. I only decided to come here this morning," I blurted out in explanation. "I have something to tell you, but first, I must apologize not only for coming uninvited but also for my outburst the last time I saw you. My rudeness was inexcusable and unprecedented."

"It may have been unprecedented but hardly inexcusable," Lady Chatsworth said. "Besides, you were completely correct. It is shameful that I have made my son so unhappy these past few years. He has done so much to try to help me be content, but I was too deep in my own misery to notice." She took both of my hands in hers and held them tightly. Her smile showed all of her straight teeth; William must have gotten his mesmerizing smile from her. More than her verbal reassurances, her nearness made me feel that I was indeed forgiven.

"I know he was happy to do everything he did for you," I said.

"No, that is not true. I don't think this marriage scheme has made him happy at all. It has made him quite miserable, and I know I rushed him on things that naturally take time. I have already told him to forget about the requirement. He can marry when the right woman for him agrees to it. I have been so happy in my marriage; I just wanted the same thing for William."

"You told him what?" If she no longer held William to that deadline, why had he come to London in order to court me? He was in no rush now.

"I told him he didn't need to be married anytime soon. I want him to be as happy as I have been in my marriage. And truthfully, it may take him some time to recover from your rejection."

"I am glad to know you're happy with Lord Chatsworth. Not all marriages are so fortunate," I said, not willing to talk about William and me yet. Her words were confusing me, and I wondered if my plan in coming here was going to backfire after all.

"Do you mean your parents? They seem happy enough," Lady Chatsworth said, surprised.

"They are happy, I suppose, individually. But together . . . I don't think they ever found love like you and Lord Chatsworth did."

"Is that why you refused William? You weren't confident you could grow to love him?"

Grow to love William? He must have done a convincing job of telling her I was the one who had refused him. Growing to love William was the least of my concerns. More than anything, I needed to start forgetting him.

"Actually, that is the reason I came to visit you." I paused and looked her up and down for any signs of ill health. "Would you mind if we sat?"

"Of course not. How could I forget my manners? I suppose I was just too surprised at seeing you." Lady Chatsworth led us over to the deep-purple velvet settee and motioned for me to sit next to her. Happy to have her sitting for what I had to say, I gritted my teeth. It was time to tell her why I had come and be done with it.

"I wanted to tell you that I never refused William. He proposed, and I accepted his proposal."

I waited for her to question me on what exactly happened, but instead, she laughed. "Oh, Rose! That is wonderful! When he told me you refused him, he was so heartbroken."

I stared at her, confused.

"No, I don't think you understand. He rejected me. I told him I would marry him, but he returned home to tell you the opposite."

"Why would he have done that?"

"The most obvious reason is that I am unsuitable. Your husband was there and actually made that quite clear."

"I don't know what happened in that garden, Rose. It sounds as though I need to talk to my husband about it, but I do know my son, and he didn't refuse you. Did you do or say anything that might have made him feel as though you didn't want to marry him?"

I was quite certain my actions during our kiss had been hard to mistake. But after the kiss . . . who had been the first one to claim that the only reason we were going to marry was because of Lady Chatsworth? Surely it was William.

He was the one who had mentioned my faults.

Which had bothered me.

It had bothered me enough that I had quickly pointed out to Lord Chatsworth that I only agreed because of Lady Chatsworth.

Could my declaration have convinced William I had no desire to marry him?

I heard a light knock, and William walked through the drawing room door. He must have kept a good pace on his walk here from the Wrights'. In his hand, he held a small pot with a dry stick rising out of the dirt inside of it. I stood up quickly enough for the blood to rush to my feet. I felt oddly self-conscious; he must have known we were just speaking of him.

"Rose," he said only slightly out of breath, "has your talk with my mother been adequate enough that I may now speak to you?" I was not certain that it had, but I nodded anyway. I stepped away from his mother and nearer to him. My mind was still wrapped around the last moment of our kiss in the garden and the resulting conversation with his father. Perhaps there were still things that needed to be cleared up.

"Good." He crossed the threshold and took four powerful steps in my direction, and we met in the center of the room. Our eyes met, and he reached for one of my hands. When he had it in his grasp, he turned it so the palm faced up and placed the pot into it. I quickly raised my empty hand and placed it over the top of William's other hand so the vessel was supported on both sides. The mischievous glint that I had seen in William's eyes during our carriage ride was still there, but when our hands touched, it seemed to grow into a fire. The fire grew hotter and more intense the longer our hands remained in contact. He slowly and carefully slid his left hand out from under my hand and removed his right hand from the top of mine. I was left holding the pot on my own. But even with our hands no longer touching, the heat from the fire was still there. With his eyes holding mine, he said, "I want to get one more thing from my chambers. I'll be right back."

After the door closed behind him, I inspected the stick and the pot closer. It wasn't a stick after all but a clipping from a rosebush. And not just any rosebush. I knew what rose clipping this was, and it seemed to solidify my newfound understanding of what had happened between us.

Over and over, I rehearsed in my mind what I must have looked like right after William had kissed me: my face covered, my declaration that the only reason we had thought to marry was because of his mother. I hadn't had time to tell him how I truly felt before his father had interrupted. The enormity of that realization, paired with my new rose, must have been showing on my face because I heard a contented sigh from across the room. I tore my gaze away from the rose to see Lady Chatsworth still sitting on the settee. The smile on her face made her look as if she were about to get everything in the world she had ever wanted.

"But what of Lord Chatsworth?" I asked. "I know he doesn't want a union between the two of us."

"You let me and William worry about Reginald. He blusters like a heavy storm cloud, but given enough time, he will settle down and become more of a light breeze," she said. I furrowed my brows at her description of her husband. I had never thought of him that way, but I hoped she was right. "Besides, the next in line to inherit is my nephew Herman, and he is a complete imbecile. He recently bought a twenty-two-year-old racehorse based on his record seventeen years prior. He paid a fortune for him and then was laughed off the track when he tried to race him." Lady Chatsworth shook her head at the memory. "Reginald already disinherited one son; I am afraid that is all the luxury the estate can afford."

William walked through the door a second time, this time holding a thick stack of diverse-sized papers in his hand. "Hello, Mother," he said with a quick glance in her direction.

"Welcome home, William. Rose has just finished telling me some very interesting information."

"I know," he said to her. "I came here to talk to her about that." William turned to me and stepped in my direction. "I have some things I want to explain to you, and I need you to hear me out completely." He stopped walking when he reached a leather club chair and placed his free hand on the back of it. "Will you hear me out?"

"I will," I said, and my answer seemed to echo like a prophecy throughout the large drawing room.

"When Joseph left," he said, "I promised myself I would never hurt my parents like he had. The one thing I learned from that episode was that one should not be selfish in love, because it affects everyone around you." I nodded in encouragement. William's never wanting to hurt his parents was no surprise to me. I wanted him to hurry and finish saying what he needed to say so he could stop bracing himself on that cursed club chair and instead come closer to me.

"Over the course of the past few weeks, I have seen my mistake," he said. "Joseph knew something I was too naïve to understand. He understood that love—real, true love—can be worth risking everything for. I could never have done what he did, not in that way, but I should have fought for you, Rose, and won a blessing from my parents. And I don't just mean that evening in the garden. I should have done it long before then." He finally pushed himself away from the chair and made his way over to me. I was still holding the pot, and he traced one finger down the length of the clipping.

"You asked me once why I tried to save the roses," he said. "I knew you loved them. That is why I tried to save them. I didn't tell you about it because I was afraid you would see how I cared for you, and I was in no position to care for you. My father had made it very clear that I had to marry the daughter of a peer, and I was too scared of tearing my family apart to defy him." He was still looking at the rose start; his eyes hadn't met mine since walking over to me. "I am not even sure if this clipping will handle a transplant. Mrs. Wright has been caring for it while I've been in London, but now it is yours. You can plant it in your home." He paused for a moment, thinking. "Or Lord Blakeley's home, wherever it will make you happiest."

"This rosebush will never be planted anywhere near Lord Blakeley's house," I said. "That man saw me more as an ornament than a person, and his concern for Adam was as fake as his wooden smile." The lines to the sides of William's mouth deepened, and the corners of his lips lifted. His eyes finally met mine.

"I had hoped that would be the case," he said.

"I'll do my best to make it grow," I told him. "Even if it means digging in the dirt." His smile deepened at the jest, but I could tell there was more he felt he needed to say.

"When Mother mentioned how happy she would be with a union between us, I was elated. But I thought I had pushed you too far away. I couldn't marry you if you were only doing it to be loyal to my mother. I wanted to, but I knew I couldn't. On top of that, my father interrupted and made my task that much more difficult." He shook his head at the memory. "I am sorry about the kiss," he said, and Lady Chatsworth reminded us of her presence with a clearing of her throat. William didn't seem to notice as he continued. "I know it was abrupt, and I am sure I scared you. I would like the chance to start slower and certainly gentler. I hope you will let me court you in earnest. Now that my mother no longer has a deadline, there would be no rush. You've been the only woman for me since I first started noticing women. I could never forgive myself if I let you go because of a misunderstanding." He reached with his free hand for my hands that were still cradling the pot but then thought better of it and placed both of his hands, papers and all, behind his back. There was nothing in my immediate vicinity for me to put my lovely rose clipping on. I was dying to set it down but didn't want to move away from William and have him misinterpret my actions once again.

"I want you to know that I *do* want to marry you for my mother's sake," he said, gesturing to his mother, who had discreetly picked up a book from the bookshelf and then proceeded to pretend to read. "But also, truly, for my sake. I fear I will never find true happiness if I don't explain everything that is in my heart now. I know I have been awful to you for the past two years. Each year, you grew more beautiful. I watched you in London as men clamored to gain your favor, and I dreaded the moment you would notice one of them. But now I hope you will notice me. I am the one clamoring like all those poor saps. Please, Rose, give me a chance to prove that I am a better man than I have been." The parlor door opened and closed. Lady Chatsworth must have given up on her book and decided to leave us alone. I really did love that woman.

"Lord Telford—" I began, and his face fell slightly. It was truly wicked of me to use his title.

"Before you answer me," he said, "I want to make one more thing clear. It is true that Mother told me I should court you but only after she saw how devastated I was at your rejection."

"But, William," I said, reverting back to his given name and stepping even closer to him. "I never rejected you."

"No," he said, rumpling his hair once again. "But you only agreed to a marriage because of your love for my mother, not for any love you have for me."

"But when you asked, I didn't reject you." Sometimes William could be a little slow, but given our history, his caution was understandable.

He did reach for my hand now, and his fingers rested softly on my own. "What are you trying to say?"

"I am trying to say that if I didn't reject you when you proposed, I think that means we are engaged."

His eyes narrowed as if he were trying to understand whether or not this was a trick, and I didn't blame him. I walked away from him and crossed the room to set the rose on a side table, then returned to him with my hands free.

"Can we just be engaged, William?" I said. "I really, really want to be engaged to you. Outside. In the garden. Preferably next to the oak tree."

His eyes widened in understanding. He took a few tentative steps in my direction and stopped just inches away from me, his worried look returning. "Is this because of my mother?" he asked.

A delighted laugh escaped my throat. Would we never be able to move past this? "I do love your mother, and I am grateful she has forgiven me after my horrible outburst, but no, William. I love you so much more than I love your mother."

"Then why . . . You looked so shaken after our kiss. I thought surely you hated me then."

"I was shaken, William, truly shaken, to the point—embarrassingly—that I couldn't look at you. But it wasn't because I didn't want you to kiss me. It was because you had."

William's hand went to cover his mouth; his fingers were splayed and pressing deeply into the skin along his cheek. I could see a sparkle in his eyes. His eyelids closed, hiding his all-knowing gray eyes from me. He inhaled deeply, and the sound of his breath was an ocean wave returning to shore. He removed his hand from his face and placed it on mine. His hand was so warm against my skin it felt as though my cheek could burst into flames. His thumb softly stroked my cheekbone.

"Do you really love me more than my mother?" he asked, tucking a stray lock of hair behind my ear.

"Much more than your mother."

"And do you love my mother very much?" He dropped the papers in his other hand, and they fluttered to the floor. He cupped my other cheek, but this time, his thumb rested on the outside of my lip.

"I do, very much," I answered, resisting the urge to press my lips into the palm of his hand.

"I haven't forgotten your request to go to the garden. That's an entreaty I'll be sure to fulfill," he said with a flash of his brilliant teeth. "But I'm going to have to do it later." He eliminated the remaining distance between us. His lips met mine, and I could feel his smile against my own. The sensation made my grin grow even larger. I traced the roughness of his cheek with my fingers, confident that this time our kiss was a beginning and not an end. Joy bubbled up from deep inside my soul until it escaped as a laugh through my otherwise occupied lips. William responded with a laugh of his own, grabbed me by the waist, and lifted me into the air. "Let's go find that oak tree!"

"William, you cannot carry me there!" I yelled as he spun me around and took a few steps toward the door without releasing me.

"Well, you can't expect me to let you go now! What if you change your mind again?"

"I never changed my mind in the first place!" I cried. I looked down at the floor and noticed the papers he had scattered around us on the floor. I squinted and tried to understand the exposed bits and pieces of the drawings. A skirt with a pattern I recognized, a young girl smiling down from the branches of an apple tree, the edge of a smiling mouth. There were dozens of them, and as far as I could tell, they were all drawings of me. "What are those drawings?" I asked.

"Oh, those," he said, glancing at them. "That's what I have been doing in my spare time for the past two years. I told you I hadn't shown you all of my drawings." A corner of one of the pictures was visible; it was my head peeking out from behind a thick and knotted wooden door. My hair was free and flowing to my waist, my eyes wide in surprise. It was the evening William had come to my room. What other moments had he captured?

"Why did you bring them now?" I asked.

"I figured if the rose clipping didn't work, perhaps my drawings could convince you that I've loved you long before that evening in the garden."

I closed my eyes in pleasure at the sound of William saying he loved me. He slowly lowered me in a movement that caused my whole body to tingle as I slid down his chest. No sooner had my feet touched the ground than he scooped me up again, this time with one arm under my legs and the other cradling my neck.

"I can't do it. I can't let you down. I am still afraid you will run away."

"I will never run away from you, William. You are the kindest man I know."

"Not for the past few years," he said with sorrow. "Not to you."

"I know," I said. "And it was killing me. I could see evidences of your kindness with your parents, neighbors, and tenants. Heavens—even Daffodil was not ignored like I was! I never could figure out what I had done to be the one person whose heart you could step on and not even notice."

"I'm so sorry," he said, nestling his face in my neck. His breath was warm and soft and too delicious for the sensitive skin on my throat to handle. When he pulled away, I released a strained breath. "I was so busy hiding my own heart, I didn't see yours."

"But you see it now."

"I see it now." He tightened his grip on me and then strode out of the drawing room and through the hall.

We reached the heavy outer door that led to the garden in no time at all. He balanced me precariously in his arms as he turned the handle and then kicked the door open. Cold air surrounded us, and the wind blew my skirt to the side.

"William, I don't even have a coat!" I exclaimed as my arms tightened around his neck.

"You will have to stay close to me, then. I'll keep you warm."

He stumbled a few times as he navigated his way to the oak tree. Just before we reached it, we passed the dry, brown, and scentless rosebushes that lay dormant for the winter. He tripped one more time as we passed them, and our laughter echoed throughout the garden. His eyes met mine, and rather than slowing down, he gathered me tighter in his arms and increased his pace.

As we reached the tree and he finally set me down, I closed my eyes and imagined the garden in the spring. The bushes would be crowned with blossoms and leaves; the scent of roses would hang in the air. The land would come alive, and the time it spent in resting would only have made it stronger.

"Are you cold?" William asked, tucking a stray strand of hair behind my ear.

I wasn't. I didn't think I would ever feel discomfort with him so near. "Yes," I lied with a wicked smile on my face. "I am very"—his smile deepened—"very cold." He licked his lips, and I bit the bottom of mine. For once, I was glad William was able to read my thoughts.

EPILOGUE

Fifteen years later—1834, London

THE NURSERY HAD PLENTY OF places to sit. Three small wooden chairs were placed near the rocking chair I sat in. A play horse and a small settee were nearby as well. But none of the children used them. Elizabeth, who was only two, sat in my lap, where she belonged. Samuel and John sat on the narrow arms of my chair. Four perpetually moving feet in wool stockings made pointing to the pictures in the book I held a sometimes impossible task. Jacob and Adam stood behind me, at times leaning in and adding another limb to the chaos.

I didn't blame them. It wasn't often I pulled out William's book of drawings.

"What's that one?" John asked, pointing at the charcoal drawing of my hand reaching for an apple.

"That is me picking an apple off the apple tree at Feldstone," I answered. "Your father and I used to climb that tree just like Adam and Jacob do now. The apples always taste best when warmed by the sun. Don't you think?"

I was stalling. It would be at least an hour before William arrived home, and I was doing anything I could to make the time go by faster.

Risking William's book to so many interested fingers was a price I was willing to pay. Samuel, who was eight, began to swing side to side, making the rocking chair rock back and forth. Rather than try to make him stop, I pushed off the floor with my feet, and we rocked back into the older two boys.

"Hey!" they cried out in unison, but we ignored them. They scrambled out of the way, and we rocked faster. Elizabeth squealed in delight, her chubby fingers reaching up and pulling some of my hair out of its chignon. Sam and John each grabbed one of my shoulders to steady themselves. The rocking chair had been a gift from Joseph and Lucinda. They had managed to bring it back with them from India after William's father had invited them home and told them they could occupy and eventually inherit Campton House. Surrey was a much closer location than India for his granddaughter to grow up. Joseph and Lucinda had returned just in time for Adam's birth, so the gift was fitting and appreciated.

My ear caught the sound of a commotion downstairs—a door slammed, and voices were raised.

Adam must have heard as well, for his head whipped around and he walked over to the door. "Father's home!" he said.

I put both feet on the ground to stop the rocking. He was home early, and I hoped that meant good news.

"Rose!" William burst through the door. His eyes were alight, almost translucent silver; even more revealing was his grin. His wide mouth showed most of his teeth as he strode to my side and picked up Elizabeth.

It passed.

I stood up and placed a kiss on his rough cheek. He pulled me into a tight hold, and Elizabeth giggled between us.

He stepped back and shifted Elizabeth so he was holding her by the waist, and then he lifted her into the air.

"It passed!" William said.

"It passed," I repeated and then flopped back down into the chair.

"What passed, Papa?" Jacob asked.

"The Chimney Sweep Act," Adam answered. "Papa has been working on passing the Chimney Sweep Act. Haven't you been listening at dinner?"

"Oh," Jacob said. "*That* passed."

"Yes," William said, stepping over to Jacob and ruffling his hair. "From now on, it is illegal for anyone under fourteen to be apprenticed to a chimney sweep. And not only that; the boys have to desire it. It cannot be forced on them."

I could tell that except, perhaps, for Adam, who had heard the story of his namesake a multitude of times, none of the children understood the magnitude of what that would mean for so many young boys around England. They had no idea what the life of a climbing boy was like. It didn't sadden me. Instead, I looked into John's sweet five-year-old eyes and hoped that the entire practice would be extinct before he was old enough to understand the enormity of what had happened today. Five years old, just one year younger than Adam had been when he had been pulled out of that chimney. The room seemed to get colder. I got out of the chair and knelt to pull John into an embrace. His warmth brightened the room again.

"You will need to write to Adam," I said. "He will want to know." Adam still lived with the Wrights when he wasn't at Cambridge.

"I wrote to him before coming home," William said. "It will be good for him to get some good news. He is happy whenever I see him, but it can't be easy for him at college. It was hard enough for me, and I started with more advantages."

There was a knock at the door, and Jane brought in a tray laden with biscuits and sweets. Behind her, Mr. Jones brought in a tray with tea. They both set their trays on the small school table and then left.

"Well, look at that," William said with a smile in his voice. "Jane has brought us some petit fours. Children, has your mother ever shown you her preferred method of eating petit fours?"

The younger children laughed, and Adam rolled his eyes.

"Four, all at once," Adam said. "Yes, Father, we know."

"Four, all at once!" William said as he reached for my waist and pulled me over to the table.

"I have never eaten petit fours four at once," I said in my primmest voice. "I do, however, feel that as a general rule, they should be eaten four in one sitting. Otherwise, why else would they be called petit fours?"

William raised his eyebrows and then looked around at our impressionable children. "Have you employed that French tutor for the children yet?" William asked.

I sucked my mouth in to prevent a smile, gave him a small salute, and said, "I will straight away." Giving up on seriousness, I reached up and brushed William's hair away from the side of his face, then stood on my toes and whispered in his ear, "Today is a remarkable day. Thank you, William. I know you worked very hard to ensure that act was passed."

"Every day with you is remarkable, Rose." He pulled me closer, but just before his lips met mine, I pulled his head to the side and softly kissed his temple. That was our kiss, our symbol that all was well, and we employed it often. William smiled at the gesture that was so familiar, pulled softly on one of my loose tendrils of hair, and then made his way to the petit fours.

ABOUT THE AUTHOR

Esther Hatch grew up on a cherry orchard in rural Utah. After high school, she alternated living in Russia to teach children English and attending Brigham Young University in order to get a degree in archaeology. She began writing when one of her favorite authors invited her to join a critique group. The only catch was she had to be a writer. Not one to be left out of an opportunity to socialize and try something new, she started on her first novel that week.